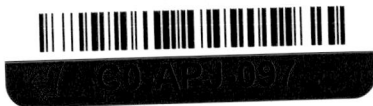

LUAG

A Time Travel Romance

JANE STAIN

www.janestain.com

ISBN 13: 978-1982962258

Available on Amazon.com

Mom made a special request that I include pictures in these books, so here you go, Mom. Love you!

This is an artist's representation of Vikings.

I've used it to label Luag's chapters, since he is from the Scottish isles and therefore comes from Viking stock.

The character Donald of Islay, Lord of the Isles is a true historic figure. Here is some of what Wikipedia has to say about him, but there is much more if you are interested:

Sometime after 1405 but before 1411, Donald gained control of Dingwall Castle, the chief seat of the earldom of Ross. In the year after the death of the nominal king, Robert III, Donald sent emissaries to England, to make contact with the heir of the Scottish throne, the captive James Stewart. King Henry IV of England sent his own emissaries to Donald in the following year to negotiate an alliance against Albany.

With control over the principal seat of the earldom of Ross and support of the exiled heir to the Scottish throne, in 1411 Donald felt strong enough to march against Albany's main northern ally, Alexander Stewart, Earl of Mar. At the Battle of Harlaw, Donald failed to inflict a decisive victory, and withdrew back to the western highlands.

Here are a few jokes about Donald's methods:

"This place is a real hidden gem. You can have it for as little as a six month siege."

"I love these Antiqueing Weekends."

Katherine is a modern girl, through and through, so here is the image used to label her chapters:

Finally, a map may help you imagine our hero and heroine's travels. The

* down near the bottom of the map along the North Channel marks Dunskey Castle, where the druid Kelsey meets with Katherine in her dreams.

@ marks the Isle of Islay, where Donald and Luag are from

A star marks Aberdeen, the setting of much of the book

\# marks Invererie, where Leif & Jessica are Laird and Lady

uag screamed. Why was Katherine on the battlefield? He lunged, grabbing her waist where she knelt between him and their enemy. He was trying to pull her away to safety even as she clung to something.

But as soon as he touched her, Luag forgot about whatever lay on the ground.

He could hear Katherine's thoughts!

"I've had enough and want to go home!" she pled in her mind while picturing the strangest place. It had large beaches but was a city of metal and glass. A pier jutted out into the ocean, and on it were brightly lit monstrosities that moved! The sign read Santa Monica Pier. Did she live in Spain, then?

Her home itself sat above an oddly bright and

cheery tavern that shared walls with two shops which were themselves squished into a row of shops in one enormous long building that faced another such building across a huge stone walkway. She couldn't see the ocean from her home, but she could smell it.

The world did flips around Luag, as if he were swimming on the seashore, being churned by the waves. Someone grabbed his back, and he lurched to get the man off him even as he held onto Katherine and pulled her away toward safety.

Abruptly, he no longer heard her mind inside his. No longer saw what she imagined. He didn't need to. He and Katherine were there, in the place she had imagined.

The ocean air was pleasantly balmy, but everything else made him uncomfortable.

He didn't understand anything he saw except the hundreds of people walking by, so for a few moments he focused on them. They were all in such a rush! And they were rude.

"Watch where you're going!"

"Get out of the way!"

"Wrong way, buddy."

"Go back to the Renaissance Faire!"

Luag would have said something back, only his

jaw hung open. They were all wearing so little clothing! Nothing was left to his imagination. The women wore even less than the men, less than undergarments. Only the briefest parts of their bodies were covered up, and he could see more skin than anything else.

None of them seemed at all bothered by it. Well, a few of the men were looking at the women, but appreciatively, not in any sort of panic that the women had lost their clothing.

These people set him on edge, and so he looked away from them.

The surface they walked on — for it could not be called the ground — was hard like stone, but flat and smooth like an earthenware plate. Everyone was walking around on it without comment, so it must've been normal for them, but it was not normal for Luag. The surface was light gray, and now that he looked closer it was marked with a series of lines that criss-crossed each other. The more he looked at it, the more aggravated he grew, overcome with the urge to bend over and scrape it away so he could see the ground.

Battle fever raged in him, preparing him to survive this encounter with the unknown. On reflex, he reached over his shoulder for his sword,

Throatfinder, cursing as he remembered taking it off to accompany Alasdair Stewart with the white flag. But there was no one to fight, no beast to kill, just too many new sounds, sights, scents, and sensations all at once.

He shifted his attention over to the right, where wheeled things moved by with startling speed on a black surface just as flat but not as smooth. Of course, the things that moved by were far more interesting than the surface. They were beautiful, made of all the colors of the precious jewels, of different metals and glass, more metal and glass than he'd seen in his whole life or ever hoped to see. What were they? Where were they going? How did they move without horses to pull them? Why did they make so much noise? Were those people he saw inside them?

He was so frustrated at not understanding what he was seeing and not knowing what things were!

And there was no place he could rest his eyes. When he glanced away from the people and the strange jeweled objects, there were only brief patches of flowers to look at before his eyes landed on one of the hundreds of buildings that loomed up all around him, blocking the view of the mountains that must surely lie beyond. Every last one of these buildings was ten times as big as Ualraig's castle. How many people must there be here in order to need so many buildings? Where was the person in charge of them? Surely he should be seeing to it they weren't so rude!

And the noise! His ears were full of hundreds of noises he didn't recognize or understand. Loud sudden noises and jarring long noises. Sound that resembled music but wasn't made of any instrument he ever heard before. The infernal noise was pervasive, and he didn't understand how everyone was ignoring it.

The place smelled bad too. The most noxious smoke ever lingered in the air, and it stung his eyes.

If all that wasn't enough, then the sight of the oddest trees imaginable pushed Luag over the edge. These trees shot up fifty feet in the air before they had any branches. Their branches were all bunched together in a ball at the top of the tree. They looked like huge skinny one-legged giants with big heads.

The only familiar thing that saved him from insanity was he was still with Katherine. And she looked calm, happy even. Obviously, she had seen all these things before and didn't consider them unusual in the least.

"I need to get back home right away," he told her, surprising himself by speaking fluent English. "This place is extremely unpleasant."

Upon hearing him and noticing he was there, she

scowled and groaned. "Aw, I finally get home and now I'm stuck with you? Why did you have to come with me?"

He took another look around just to assure himself it really was as odd as he had thought. "Och, this is your home? No wonder you traveled back in time." With all this change, it pleased him that some of the words he said at least were still familiar. Apparently, whatever magic had allowed the lasses to speak Gaelic in his time was also allowing him to speak English in hers, but it left his accent and a few colorful words in his speech, and he appreciated that.

Katherine groaned again, and this time it was more like a growl. "What am I going to do with you?" Startling him, she grabbed his waist and pulled him into the shade of a tree.

"What are you—"

"My pest of a neighbor's looking out her window. I don't want her to ask where I've been. Trust me, it's better that way. Besides, I don't have any men's clothes for you. Come on."

Unaccustomed to women touching him —as were all unmarried men of his time— he lurched with shock as she grabbed him by the hand and tugged him along the odd wide walkway. She took him through a door made entirely of glass into a shop full of the scant clothing everyone wore.

"You aren't going to wear this clothing, Katherine!"

Laughing at him, she grabbed the first few things she saw amid all this decadent plenty and dragged him to the back wall where three doors stood. "Try this on for size and show me how it fits."

He balked.

"Now."

Rather amused by bossy Katherine but trying his best not to show it, he did as he was told. The room was no more than a closet, but it had a convenient bench where Luag put his leather tunic, linen shirt, and woolen knee breeches. It also had an exquisite mirror, clear as water. He had never seen himself so well before and couldn't help staring. Unlike all the other people around here, his skin was scarred in dozens of places from the hundreds of small skirmishes he'd been in throughout his 25 years.

Katherine's voice came impatiently under the gap beneath the door. "Get out here so I can see you!"

"I'm working on it. It's just I have never seen clothing like this before." He stood staring at the strange fastening on the scandalously short pants. Shrugging, he tried brute force — and was surprised when it worked. With a sound as if he had snapped his thumb across his middle finger, the odd trousers opened.

A few minutes later he opened the door and stepped out of the little room, certain he would find her red-faced with embarrassment at his state of undress.

"Ye asked for it, lass."

She scoffed, handing him one of two brightly colored rucksacks. "Here, I'm sure you'll need your other clothes when you go back home, and I'll sell mine. Lauren says handmade historical costuming like this costs a small fortune."

But the clothing she wore had belonged to a dear friend's mother. He wouldn't allow her to sell it. Out loud, he only said "thank you" as he took the rucksack she handed him and put his things in it.

"Come on over here," she said, standing in front of a wall filled with those useless strappy shoes everyone wore here. "While I get changed, you find some sandals that fit."

Dutifully, Luag looked at the holey shoes. How would he sheath his sgian-dubh in one of those? No. He'd keep his boots on. His sgian-dubh was the only weapon he had with him.

He glanced around and was drawn to an exquisite glass case in the center of the shop. Inside were many items he didn't understand, but something called a Swiss Army Knife grabbed his attention and wouldn't let go.

"Would you like to see it up close?" Asked a man his age behind the case.

"Aye."

Smiling, the man placed the Swiss Army Knife down on the top of the glass case. "It has all the normal attachments," he said matter-of-factly, and then he swiveled each attachment out as he spoke of it. "Large blade, small blade, scissors, tweezers, screwdriver, corkscrew, nail file." And then he got an excited tone in his voice. "But it has some new things as well. Thumb drive most importantly, but also there's this handy solar charger."

Luag was salivating. He had no idea what those last two special things were, but scissors! Corkscrew! Tweezers! This was an amazing piece of equipment. "I want it. Now we only need tae do the bargaining."

The other men laughed.

Remembering what Katherine had said, Luag pulled his clothing out of the rucksack and told the man, "All this can be yours for only the price of that Swiss Army knife." He smiled and waited for the man to readily agree.

But the man laughed again. "Nice try, but I'm not into that Renaissance Faire stuff. The only way you're getting this," he scooped the knife up and clutched it in his fist, but held it up so Luag could see it, "is if you pay me the ninety-nine ninety-nine it says clearly on the price tag."

Luag made himself laugh the way the other man had. "For a moment there, I thought you meant 99 gold, but obviously you just mean 99 silver."

Luag was digging around in his bag for his money when that odd music came from the man's trousers

The man took out a small glass box, looked at it, shrugged, tapped it, and put it to his ear! And then he spoke into it. "No, I'm not really busy. Just helping some gaming nerd. Wants to buy a Swiss Army Knife but talks about giving me gold for it." He rolled his eyes!

Normally, Luag didn't do business with shopkeepers who were so rude. But he wanted that knife. Finally having dug out one of the 10 gold coins he possessed, he plopped it on the counter. "Ninety-nine silver. Sold." He held out his hand for the knife.

The shopkeeper's rude apprentice groaned. "We don't take foreign currency. You'll have to go the bank and exchange it." He gave Luag a hopeful look. "Unless you have a Visa or MasterCard?"

Luag pondered this. Did they have servant cards as well? What did these cards do, if little glass boxes could make them communicate with people?

Katherine's voice came up beside him, and she

was wearing a perfume now that was exquisite, making him inhale deeply with bliss. "Is there a problem?" She asked the apprentice, of all people.

"This your friend?" the man asked Katherine. When he got a good look at her, he put his glass box away so he could pay her more attention.

She looked at Luag with mischief, her eyes saying, "See how much you depend on me?" But she told the man, "I wouldn't call him a friend, more like a pesky relative, but yeah, he's staying with me, and no, he's not from around here."

The apprentice never took his eyes off Katherine, and he fidgeted with the Swiss Army Knife while he blathered on with a foolish smile on his face. "Well tell him he can't use foreign currency here. Better yet, help him sign up for a credit card. He's going to need one if he does any shopping at all, or eats at a restaurant, or even takes a cab. Well, you know. How long is he staying?"

Luag thought of an excuse for them to leave. "Let's go" he said to her. "I'm in need of some food."

Giving Luag an odd little smile, she handed the shopkeeper a card and then grabbed a tiny scrap of parchment attached to Luag's odd new tight-fitting tunic and reached it out to the man, who waved over it something that chirped like a bird.

"All these clothes," she said to the shopkeeper,

"the sandals that came in this box, and throw in that knife, too." She said the part about the knife with a shrug, throwing Luag a superior smile that said, 'You owe me now.'

2

Katherine drank in the sights and sounds of the 2nd Street Promenade as they left Old Navy. Had she really been gone a year? These clothes weren't her style, but Luag wasn't going to be here long enough to warrant a trip to Beverly Hills on his behalf. The two of them would fit in now, instead of looking like starving actors advertising their show. That was all she'd meant to accomplish with this clothing purchase.

Staying close to the shops on the same side of the Promenade as her apartment in order to avoid the beady eyes of her loudmouth neighbor, she made her way down to the cafe beneath her apartment. She simply had to have a nonfat cinnamon latte, and they had pastries for Luag's stomach. Why had he grabbed onto her when she was wishing she could go home? His being here nearly ruined it for her.

She had no doubt Lauren's druid friend, Kelsey, could find a way to get Luag back to his time, but she didn't want to wait a month for Kelsey to contact her in her dreams. That University she'd gone to — where they'd made her a druid without her realizing it— kept her busy. She could only visit Lauren and her friends once a month or so.

Ooh! Maybe Kelsey's email address or even her cell number was on that University's website. Katherine would look Kelsey up once they got to the café and she could charge her phone. She had taken so many pictures back in the 1400s that it was dead. Mostly of Jessica's wedding.

Something in a jewelry store window caught Katherine's eye as she passed by.

She gasped. Was that the new Alberto Milani ring? She pushed her whole body up against the window so that it blocked the sun and she could read the label on the box. It was! Shaking with excitement, she pushed her way through the heavy glass doors into the shop and found a salesperson.

"Can I see that new Alberto Milani ring, please? Size 6."

Annoyingly, Luag had followed her into the store and was standing there frowning. As usual, he didn't like something she'd done. "You know I hunger," he said, "yet you stop to buy trinkets?"

"It's the new Alberto Milani," she told him before she realized he wouldn't even know who that was. Ugh, he was so tiring. She paid for and wore the ring, which reminded her about Luag's new Swiss Army Knife. She handed him its box and threw the shopping back away.

With a sheepish grin, he took the knife out of its box and slid its sheath onto the belt of his new walking shorts.

Soon, they were once more on their way to the food he'd said he wanted.

"Katherine?"

"Yeah?" She turned to look at his surprisingly earnest face.

"Will you help me get one of those master cards so that I can buy things too?" The hopeful tone in his voice was kind of endearing despite how annoying he could be.

She laughed. "You actually have to have money to pay those."

"I have money," he said, reaching for his backpack.

She threw her hands up. "Anyway, we're getting you home, so you won't need a MasterCard."

The smile he gave her at that was even more

hopeful, and she smiled, herself, in relief. Good, she would be rid of him soon.

The coffee aroma hit her twenty feet from the door of the café.

She breathed in deep, savoring the taste she'd missed for a year. It was midmorning, and the place was crowded. Spotting an empty outlet, she pointed it out to Luag. "Quick, go save that thing on the wall while I get our food." She used the sign language the two of them both knew well from playing Charades together for a year, so that no one would overhear it. She almost gave him her phone to plug in, but thought better of it. Who knew what trouble someone from the Middle Ages would get into trying to harness electricity? She shuddered.

Using the same sign language, he said he would do as she asked. Only, he used the warrior signal for guarding it, rather than the Charades signal for saving it, which puzzled her at first.

It was kind of fun watching him skulk over there like the warrior he was while she stood in line to give her order to the barista. The amount of caution he used! To her, this cafe was like an extension of her upstairs apartment, she spent so much time here. His caution reminded her that he was out of his element the same way she had been when she first arrived in 1410 Scotland and met him in Inverurie.

Despite the contempt she had for him as someone who could never approve of anything she did, she felt the tiniest bit of sympathy for Luag, knowing just how bad his culture shock certainly was.

And then she giggled at seeing him sit down and just watch everyone warily. Anyone else would be on their phone.

In fact, while she watched, several people approached him.

"Hey buddy, you going to use that outlet?"

She giggled harder at their reactions when Luag gave them the sternest look they'd probably ever seen in their lives.

The good news was Kelsey had indeed paid Katherine's bills as she'd promised. Her cards were working just fine. She'd used two different ones at Old Navy and the jewelry store. Getting out a third one, she finally approached the barista.

Lupe's face lit up, and she started Katherine's nonfat cinnamon latte immediately. "Where have you been for a whole year, Chica?"

Katherine gave Lupe her signature nose wrinkle and her level seven smile, saying "Scotland" as if it were no big deal.

Lupe made an impressed face while routinely saying, "Anything else?" as if she didn't expect a yes.

"Yeah," Katherine perused the pastry case. "One of those slices of cheesecake." Her stomach growled, reminding her she hadn't eaten since last night.

The barista laughed "You don't look like you changed your eating that much in Scotland."

Katherine laughed a little too. "Of course not. Give me two forks." She used this opportunity to glance over and make sure Luag was still doing okay.

Still on high alert, he started to get up, signing to her, "Do you need help?"

"No, stay there," Katherine quickly signed back.

He sat back down, but his eyes scanned the area around her.

Lupe made an appreciative clicking noise. "No wonder you spent so long in Scotland. He's one of your models, no? He's a good one. I wouldn't mind trying out survival gear with him."

Katherine didn't correct her. It was a good cover story, so she just let it stick. "Thank you," she said with a smile as Lupe handed her a tray with the cheesecake slice and her latte.

"Aren't you going to get your guapo something to drink?"

"He doesn't drink coffee. But yeah, please give me a big water for him, and thanks."

As soon as Katherine plugged her phone in, it went nuts.

You have 6,973 notifications.

She spent the next few minutes sending mass texts, explaining to all her contacts she was fine and she would catch up with them later.

She checked her employer's website to see the new products they'd put out during the last year. Wow, it would be fun selling that James-Bond-style underwater breather. And those working cell-phone earrings. Wow, she would have to drop by the shop asap and get a pair of those.

Against her will, she imagined Luag modeling PenUlt's new survival knapsack, made of genuine cowhide. Lupe was right, it would look so good on him up on a mountain in the Highlands...

Now now. Get your mind away from the impossible and back to the task at hand: getting rid of Luag.

She downloaded a book about the history of Luag's town, Inverurie. Hoping it would give her ideas on how to get him home, she put in one of her ear buds so she could listen to it, offering the other to Luag.

It was more fun watching his reactions than listening to the book. His eyes popped open wide when the narration started, and he kept grinning or gritting his teeth at what was said about the town where his best friend Leif was laird.

They were on Chapter 6 when Lupe waved as she left the café. "See you soon, Chica. Si?"

Katherine raised up her nonfat cinnamon latte in salute to the woman who made them perfectly. "See you tomorrow!"

Lupe smiled as she left.

Taking a sip of the delectable drink, Katherine was so glad she'd come home at last. She fired up the browser on her phone and searched for Kelsey MacGregor. Encouraged at seeing a number of hopeful possibilities, she clicked on the first one.

But the outlet was awkwardly far away from the table, making her block the aisle with her cord, now that she was holding her phone up to look at it. Afraid someone would trip, she got up and stood against the wall.

Luag was moving next to her when a man looking at his phone ran into Katherine.

"Excuse me, I didn't see you—"

Luag got in the man's face. "You will apologize to the lass!"

Katherine put her hand on Luag's wrist, trying to get his attention. "It was an honest mistake."

But Luag continued staring at the man, nostrils flaring and fists clenching.

She noticed that everyone had stopped what they were doing to watch the spectacle.

Wearing a barista apron, a man she didn't know came over and stood behind Luag. "Sir, you need to leave. Now." He gave Katherine an apologetic look. "Sorry, ma'am, store policy. We don't allow customers to speak to each other that way."

Katherine nodded at the barista, picked up what was left of her latte, put her phone in her bag, and grabbed Luag by the wrist, dragging him out the door. Once they were outside, she dragged him around the corner.

Away from her neighbor's prying eyes and ears, she lit into him. "You cannot act that way in this time!"

"Me act a certain way! He was manhandling you!"

"He was on his phone and didn't see me. It happens all the time."

"It shouldn't happen at all, and to hear you say it happens all the time makes me wonder why you want to be in this time!"

"This time is far more enlightened as to women's independence than your time!"

Luag's face turned crazed. "You want to be independent? Fine!" He ran down the sidewalk toward the cliff over the ocean two blocks away.

"Good riddance," Katherine said to herself. She'd had more than enough of his superior take-charge attitude this past year. The man was insufferable. Halfway up to her apartment, she decided to call PenUlt and tell them she was back and would come in tomorrow to once more be their top salesperson.

She dug out her keys and went inside. There was so much to do! Make sure she had something to wear tomorrow, coax the salon into a haircut and manicure on short notice... Good thing Luag had run off. She needed this whole afternoon to get ready. But first things first. She was going to take a hot bath. She'd missed those even more than lattes.

L uag ran as far as he could toward the sea before hitting a wooden rail fence on the edge of a cliff. There had to be a way down there. He turned to his right and ran along the grassy park with its odd small buildings. Before long, he came to a hill covered in that same black stuff. Jeweled monstrosities sped up and down at those impossible speeds, but there was a white area on the left for people. He followed the crowd until at last he was on the edge of all this madness, staring out at the breaking waves.

Amid all the people walking up and down the shoreline, he thought he saw someone familiar. But that was impossible.

He put the Swiss Army knife and his sgian-dubh in his sporran, gripped that in his teeth, left his boots in the sand, and waded into the blessedly cool water. In addition to everything else, this place was unbearably hot. It felt good to swim in the sea. He hadn't played in the surf since he was a child on Islay.

However, before too long his stomach growled. With no line to catch a fish and no ember to light a cooking fire, he had to face the fact that he was helpless here. He needed to go beg forgiveness from the lass. He walked around barefoot in the dry sand until the wet sand had all dried and fallen off his feet, put his boots back on, and headed back to Katherine.

When he was wondering which of the four doors belonged to her, a little old gammer came up and took hold of his elbow. This made him jump, half out of being startled and half out of amazement that a woman would touch a stranger. But her face and voice were both sweet when she spoke.

"I live in number three and Katherine lives in number two. I'm sure she'll forgive you if you give her the chance. Go on up there. I just heard her run a bath a little while ago, so I know she's at home. It would be a shame to let young love like yours go to waste."

Luag smiled at the old woman. Katherine must've meant a different neighbor was a pest. This one was a delight. "Thank you," he told her before he rushed on up the stairs.

"You're welcome, young man. You're very welcome here."

He was smiling at the woman's kindness even as he wondered what he was going to say to Katherine, and then he realized who that familiar face belonged to, the one he saw down near the sea. It was Roland Cheyne, one of the men on the enemy side at the white-flag talk on the battlefield. A new addition to his uncle's clan, not anyone Luag had known.

It must have been Roland who grabbed hold of Luag and came here with them.

If Roland meant Katherine harm...

The door flew open and Katherine dragged him inside and slammed it.

Luag felt saliva pool in his mouth. The sight of her stirred him like nothing ever had before.

Not only had she taken a bath and brushed her lovely hair out so that it fell down to her waist in blonde waves, she had also changed clothes, if you could call it that. She wore what would in his time not even be an undergarment, a pretty sleeveless pastel pink shift that didn't even cover her knees. And those shoes she had on. How did she walk in heels so high?

She started off shrewish. "What were you thinking, running off like that?" And then she met his eyes. "Sorry my pesky neighbor bothered you. She really does stick her nose in everyone's business. Did you hear her saying how she knew I was in the bath?" She shuddered. "Creepy!"

Throughout this short speech, she was behaving as if her clothing were normal, and so he did his best not to stare at the barely concealed charms of this lass he had known a year, instead looking around the room.

Her rucksack containing Leif's mother's heirloom clothing had been casually tossed into a corner, and she didn't stop him when he went over and transferred the clothing that now belonged to Leif's new wife, Katherine's friend Jessica, into his own rucksack.

"These things were Leif's mother's, ye ken."

She gave him a sad smile. "Aye, you should take them back to him."

"One of Laird Donald's men followed us here. I saw him on the beach."

Her face brightened. "Maybe he can get you home!"

Luag shook his head in disbelief. "He was sent by a man who means harm, Katherine. We canna trust him." He looked around her home, and though it was foreign to him, at least most of it made sense. Seeing what vaguely looked like a kitchen, he turned to her. "Before, I was merely hungered, now I am in serious danger of fainting if I dinna have food."

She sighed. "Yeah, me too." She smiled in eager anticipation. "We'll go to my favorite place."

"Nay, it isn't safe for you to leave, not with Donald's man out there." Luag moved in front of her door to bar the way. And was shocked when she marched right up and tried to push him aside!

"I've been gone a year," she said. "There's not a thing in here fit to eat. Come on. It's close, and there so many people out there, what's he going to do?"

Only the growling of his stomach persuaded him. Besides, if he was with her, she should be all right. He'd already sheathed his sgian-dubh back into his boot, and now he put the Swiss Army Knife back on the belt of his strange new loose breeches.

There were indeed many people walking here, clamoring, shouting, and looking at their glass boxes while they rushed to and fro.

The place she took him to was only half a mile's walk, and he was reassured when they entered an upstairs tavern. Reassured, that is, until nothing on the menu looked familiar in any way. She ordered for him, and when his food came, it was completely foreign.

His stomach growled again, so taking a big drink of the watery stuff that passed for ale here, he tried a bite. It was surprisingly good, but he wouldn't tell her that.

She wasn't deceived, however. Smiling brightly, she said, "I'm so glad you like sushi, too."

That smile did something to him. He felt drawn to her unexpected warmth and gave her a tentative smile of his own. This kept getting better and better throughout the meal.

But when they arose to leave, he saw Roland again. The small man was seated near the exit, dressed in the strange loose breeches and tight-fitting tunic of these times.

The battle heat came upon Luag, and he reached for his sgian-dubh.

Sense overtook him before he had drawn it. Katherine was right. The little man wouldn't do anything inside this crowded place.

"Don't look over toward the door," he told Katherine, "howsoever, Donald's man Roland Cheyne is over there waiting for us to leave so he can follow us. So you leave alone. I want to see if he follows you without me along."

She flashed him a look so afraid it melted his heart.

"Dinna fash," he rushed to tell her, "I will be right behind him."

She nodded and did as he told her.

Roland followed the lass out.

Luag cursed and ran out after the smaller man. As soon as all three of them were in the staircase, he pinned Roland against the wall. With his sgian-dubh to the man's throat. He told Katherine, "Go back inside. Don't let anyone come out here until I call you."

She nodded and went.

He turned back to Roland. "What are you doing here?"

Roland's body was slack. The man wasn't resisting at all. In fact, he was trembling, and his eyes were crazed, desperate. "Donald sent me after the other lass's dagger, but I sensed you were going to the future. I can only go where someone has been. I wanted to ride along. Just for a look, mind. I thought I would go right back and grab the dagger a second later. But the moment I arrived in this time filled with the work of men, I became helpless to reach Mother Nature. I can't even sense her!" Hope came into Roland's eyes. "But the lass! She has visions of places even here where Nature yet reigns. I will do anything you ask, just allow the lass to get me back to Nature."

Roland could time travel! Luag re-sheathed his sgian-dubh and looped the druid's arm through his own, ostensibly to help him down the stairs. "Katherine, come on out!"

A moment later, she appeared, laughing and talking with a large group of people.

Luag hurried Roland down the stairs and out of their way.

"So," she said, looking expectantly from Luag to Roland and back to Luag. "I see Roland has joined us. What's the plan? I'm sure you have one. I can see it in your eyes."

Luag answered in their silent Charades language, lest anyone overhear. "Roland is a druid who can time travel. He will take me back home, but first you need to get us away from all this man-made settlement to where he can feel the power of Nature. Let's go."

But Katherine scoffed. "Are you kidding me? It's Friday evening!" She looked at him as if he were daft.

Luag raised his chin at the insult, but just in case she had a point, he asked, "And why does that make any difference?"

Katherine grimaced, but on her it looked lovely, just as everything did. When had he noticed that? She put her hand up in a gesture of peace. "I keep forgetting you two don't know LA. It would take us all night to get out of town right now."

"You've got that right," said a passerby who reached up.

Katherine slapped his raised hand.

The man just shook his head with a smile and kept on walking by.

She said, "Tomorrow morning it will be smooth sailing, so we need to stay here tonight." She looked at Roland. "Have you eaten?"

Timidly, Roland shook his head no.

Katherine growled in frustration, but then flung her hand to the side. "It doesn't matter. The Miramar has room service. Come on."

Keeping hold of Roland's arm, Luag followed her. "The Miramar is the local inn?"

She nodded but didn't look at him, intent on her destination.

"Why an inn? Why not just go back to your home? It's plenty big for three. I've known families of ten who had smaller homes."

She raised her eyebrows at him and then turned back in front of them, rushing along the large walkway surrounded by shops. "That may be, but even in my time, a single woman does not bring two men home with her. Not with a neighbor like mine, she doesn't. I'd never hear the end of it. No, we're going to the Miramar. Room service, and they'll have toothbrushes for you and... Just trust me, we're better off there."

They rounded a corner toward the sea and went down the street a ways.

"There it is, the Miramar," she said with the sort of fondness most people reserved for their homes.

Luag looked over at Roland and was pleased to see the man was just as flabbergasted as he was. This inn was larger than any castle he'd seen, except the one in Edinburgh.

Smiling superiorly, Katherine led them inside, where it seemed even bigger, with ceilings several stories tall like in a cathedral, but all in white. Katherine got a key from one of ten lasses sitting behind a large desk and took them inside a tiny room whose doors opened by magic. "Brace yourselves," she said. And then, laughing, she pushed on a glass panel in the wall.

The room moved! Luag could feel movement, as if he were on a horse that ran uphill. But the room moved far faster. So much faster that if Katherine hadn't told him to brace himself — and if he hadn't listened to her — he would've fallen to the floor.

The magic doors opened and it was different outside than it had been before. A window showed only sky and clouds.

Gawking, Luag asked her, "Can it possibly have..."

Nodding, she led them out of the small room and up to the window. "Yep. That tiny little room moved us up 15 floors."

Luag felt like he was flying. He could see the ocean and that pier with the carnival rides in front of him, and to the side buildings stretched out as far as he could see. He would have gladly stood there gawking all night, but Roland started to keel over, so Luag resentfully dragged the smaller man away from the window.

Katherine led them down the carpeted hallway, which was lit by more gold sconces, stopped in front of a door, and used the key she'd gotten to open it, then gestured for them to precede her inside.

Still holding Roland's arm, Luag entered the cavernous inn room.

Katherine picked up what looked vaguely like a large seashell. "Make yourselves at home. I know I plan to. If you need anything at all —food, blankets, towels, ice, what-have-you— just pick up this thing here and push the button that says 'Front Desk,' then hold it to your mouth and ear like this and talk. They will help you."

4

Katherine smiled in relief to be in a suite at the Miramar. This was much more like it. She deserved some first-class treatment after the year she'd had: cold-water sponge baths. She had to admit though, the food had all been delicious. You just couldn't beat homemade meals with farm-fresh ingredients.

She clicked the TV on, made herself an espresso martini at the bar, and plopped down on the L-shaped sectional, complete with a floating section to put her feet up on. "Ah, this is the life I missed."

It was just the news on TV, but having missed a year's worth, she found it comforting. Earthquakes, fires, tornadoes, and crime all over the world. She laughed. "The celebrity gossip's just icing on the cake!"

Maybe it was mean of her, being their hostess and all, but she didn't lift a finger to help the men adapt. No, she just sat there with her feet up and watched TV, chuckling at their foibles.

"Hello, Front Desk. Verra pleased I am to meet you. I am Luag MacDonald. ... Verra well, I'll get on with it. Can we have some food here, please? ... Do you have anything from Scotland? ... Aye, that sounds verra good. ... I thank you. We look forward to sampling some of your cooking."

A few minutes later.

"Hello, Front Desk. I am Roland Cheyne. Pleased I am to make your acquaintance . ... Verra well, there are only two beds in this room, and there are three of us, all unmarrit. Is the third person expected to sleep on the floor — not that I'm complaining, mind ... I dinna see a door. ... Ah, there it is."

A door opened.

A gasp.

Roland's voice coming from the next room. "Och, aye! This will do verra nicely. I thank you for your warm hospitality...."

Her phone had been buzzing all afternoon, and now she finally got back to it.

Mom: Got any photos of the Celtic Rock musician you toured with?

Katherine: No, but it's over, and I'm home.

Mom: Ooh! Can I come see you?

Katherine: Yes, but wait a few days. I have company.

Mom: A new someone special, I hope.

Katherine: No, no one special.

Mom: Are you sure?

Katherine: Yes, I'm sure. Just people I met on my trip. They tagged along home with me for a free place to stay.

Mom: I hope you're being careful.

Katherine: Yes, of course I am.

And then Roland was wailing, "My grove. I need to be in my grove. Tending my trees. I can't hear them. They can't be all gone. All my trees!"

At first, Katherine ignored the man, hoping he would stop or fade into mumbles.

But no. "They've murdered all my trees! All the trees! It's so silent!"

The man needed sedation, and looking over at the bar, she saw the means within reach. So she went over and gathered all the scotch she could find, and then all the whiskey. Heck, she threw the rum in as well. Mini bar bottles cost what, ten dollars each? Well worth it. She poured them all into one pitcher, threw in some ice, and stirred it up.

With a sympathetic face, she offered it to the wailing man. "Here. You look like you could use this."

It worked. Roland absentmindedly took the pitcher by the handle and gulped down some of the potent cocktail. Then some more. The more he drank, the more talkative he became — but also less whiny, thank God.

"I will convince my druid brothers to save our precious groves o' trees. I will na help Donald turn Scotland into this monstrous unnatural type o' place, no I will na."

Katherine felt a thrill go through her at this. "This is wonderful news, Luag!"

"How do you figure that, lass?"

"Don't you see? Roland will tell the other druids about the damage world domination does to nature and then they'll call off the whole war!"

But Roland's face wrinkled up in sadness. "Donald was gaun'ae march on Scotland regardless o' us druids."

Katherine gave Luag a look, trying to share a moment where they agreed Roland was off his rocker. But to her shock, his face agreed with the little man. A distinctly highlander determination accompanied this agreement, and for a moment, all she could do was admire him. But that moment passed quickly.

She used their Charades hand signals to ask him behind Roland's back, "Why don't you look surprised?"

His eyes said, "Oh, come on," while his hands signaled, "Everyone knew the Laird o' the Isles coveted the region when he chose his bride. This is the reason Leif has been training the militia extra hard. He has been expecting this war."

Toward the end of the pitcher, Roland said something that changed Katherine's mind about going back with the two of them to the 1400s.

"Your friends are in grave danger. Even now, Donald marches on Aberdeen. We druids hae seen that Donald, as Scotland's king, will make the kingdom a world power. I am na longer gaun'ae help him. I now see what being a world power does to our precious groves o' trees, the poor darlings! Howsoever, I will na be able to stop Donald. I only hope I can convince my druid brothers to save the trees!"

The druid broke down into sobs.

Over his bowed head, Katherine signed to Luag, "Help him into the other room, put him to bed, and hope he falls asleep and gives us some quiet."

Leif signaled "I thought the bedroom was yours."

Opening her eyes as wide as she could to emphasize that this warranted a change of plans, she signed back to him, "You and I can sleep out here on these two arms of the couch."

"Very well," Luag signed back just before doing as she said and escorting the now woozy and stumbling Roland into the bedroom.

Katherine had vague fears of the man peeing the bed or something similar, but surely the fine wouldn't be too high. And it would be worth it to have him off their hands.

Luag came back into the suite's living room just as there was a knock at the door.

"Room service!"

The waiter left the table in front of the couch.

Luag dug in with enthusiasm at first, grabbing the bread and meat together in Medieval fashion. But he stopped with a disgusted look on his face after just one bite. "This isna Scottish food."

Katherine picked up her fork and daintily demonstrated proper 21st Century manners. "Of course it isn't. You're in the USA, not in Scotland. This is our version of your fare."

He watched her use her fork for a minute and then tried it. He did pretty well, only fumbling once.

While they ate, Katherine watched a never-ending series of surprises on the news. Stealing a sidelong glance at Luag, she saw that he was watching too. His eyes were so big with amazement that she was impressed he was able to keep on eating. It softened her heart. Back in his time, he had seemed so arrogant, so smug. She liked this naïve and surprised look on his face.

They were watching a commercial with several businessmen shaking hands with each other, and it gave her an idea. "I've changed my mind. I'm coming with you back to your time. I can't abandon Lauren and Jessica — or Amy, for that matter. Just promise me something."

Luag gave her a wary look as he sipped from his bottle of craft beer. "I need to know the promise first, lass."

"Fair enough. The next time you get exasperated with me because I don't know something that everybody knows, you'll remember how you feel right now watching TV — something everybody knows around here and has done their whole lives. Do we have a deal?"

He smiled. "Aye, we have a deal."

She reached out her hand to shake, and slowly at first, then with more determination, he shook it. She thought they held hands longer than strictly necessary for a handshake, but she didn't want to let go either.

At long last she did let go so that she could pick up the room phone and call the front desk. "Yes, please get us an Uber up to Big Bear in the morning. ... Hm. Send us a variety of breakfast foods at eight and ask the Uber to be here at nine. ... Thanks. And I'm emailing you a list of other items I'd like delivered to our room along with breakfast."

5

Luag dreamt Katherine had schemed somehow to be his wife. She had bargained for him and won, and he had to live with her. Be nice to her. Dote on her. Leif and Taran thought it was the best arrangement possible, as she was friends with their wives, and the six of them were rearing Leif and Taran's younger sister Amena together.

His eyes popped open. A ray of sunshine had come through the gap between the odd tapestries that hung in front of the windows. Good thing. Roland likely had to relieve himself, and Katherine had muttered something about a fine for any damage to the bed. And speaking of Katherine, she smelled so nice, like roses touched by a summer rain.

Wait, why could he smell her?

There was movement around his head, why?

Oh no.

What he had thought was a pillow was actually Katherine. She was curled around his head like one cat around another.

Slowly, oh so slowly, he lifted her arms off his shoulders. No need to wake her just yet. It was so peaceful and quiet without her talking. Holding his breath, he got up, watching her peaceful sleep — just for the slightest sign he had disturbed her and needed to run, mind.

He went into the other room to check on his prisoner. The druid was awake, and badly in need of relieving himself, just as Luag had suspected. Roland wasn't quite straining yet against the bonds that tied him to the bed, but Luag could tell he was close.

Silently, Luag cut the bonds and escorted the small man into the bathroom. He'd seen some very eye-opening stories last night on what Katherine called the TV, and he showed Roland how to operate the toilet and the shower, then trapped him in the bathroom by dragging the heavy dresser in front of the door. The druid was so blocked from magic that there was no way he'd be able to get out.

Secure in that knowledge, Luag used the other toilet and the other shower, all the while marveling at how easy it was when the water came to you, rather than you going to get water. And this water was hot! Eager as he was to get home and warn his friends about Donald's imminent plan to raid Aberdeen, he could get used to this.

Katherine was awake by the time he finished dressing. She had been into the bedroom and seen the dresser in front of the bathroom door, because her face was a bit stricken. To her credit, she didn't comment on it.

She brushed by him on her way into the bathroom. "I see you've already showered. Good. Breakfast and some other things I ordered will come in a few minutes. Would you please let the man in when he comes with them? Go ahead and eat. I'll grab a quick bite once I'm done in the shower."

Curious what she'd had sent, he raised his eyebrows and nodded her into the bathroom. He let Roland stay in the other bathroom until after both the food and Katherine's things had arrived. One of them was a masterfully crafted leather satchel.

The breakfast was amazingly variable, but like all food here, it tasted a little... bland. He couldn't put his finger on the reason why, but the milk had barely any flavor to it, and neither did the eggs. They filled his stomach though, and so he shrugged it off.

The telephone rang and Katherine answered.

"Okay, go ahead and check us out, and we'll be right down."

Luag resisted the urge to stare at the vast expanse of the open ceilings on the way out, but it was difficult because they seemed even more grand in the daylight than they had at sunset the day before.

Out the front door, they were greeted by one of those jeweled monstrosities complete with a stranger to drive it. He was standing on the smooth walking surface beside the machine chewing something but not swallowing it. The monstrosity had doors, and they were all wide open.

The most disturbing thing was that hideous music came out of the monstrosity, loud and thumping and frightening.

"Hello! I'm Gregory, but you can call me Greg. Going to Big Bear, huh? No luggage? Oh, can I take your bag?" The young MacGregor held out his hand to Luag for his knapsack.

Not wanting to offend, Luag looked at Katherine and signed, "Is it the custom for me to give him this bag? Because I don't want to."

She signed back, "Tell him you'll command it."

Luag mustered what smile he could and told the man, "I'll command it," in as serious a tone as he could manage, just so the man would know he meant it.

But the man raised his hands in the air in mock surrender. "Suit yourself. All right ma'am, I think you should sit in front," he said, helping Katherine into one of the doors. "And you sirs can sit in the back." He gestured for them to get in.

Just like he'd seen on the TV last night, Luag put Roland into the vehicle, putting a hand on top of his head to keep him from suing anyone, as Katherine had explained. After slamming the door shut with a satisfying bang that made Roland wince, Luag rushed around to the other side and got in before the druid could get out, rather pleased with himself for handling it so smoothly.

And then the man who had called himself Greg and so must be a MacGregor got in. "Fasten your seatbelts, gentlemen."

Not knowing what he meant, Luag looked to Katherine.

Licking her lips, she leaned into the back from the front of the vehicle. Looking first at the seat and then at Luag, she grabbed some things on the seat to either side of him, held them up in front of his sporran, and then rammed them together with a snapping sound. "You fasten Roland's seatbelt," she told Luag.

But the little man had been watching and got it done by himself.

MacGregor started the engine.

Luag spent the next two hours with a white-knuckle grip on the seat in front of him. How were there so many of these jeweled monstrosities? And so much smooth white surface. How did they go so fast? How did Katherine stand this music?

Gradually, they left the city and re-entered nature, as Katherine had promised. They'd been going up a winding road onto a mountain with trees and flowers and plenty of other foliage for quite a while when Roland spoke up.

"I know I told you I'd take you back with me," he said to Luag in a whisper, "but my druid kindred will be gloriously angry with me—"

"I'm not letting go," Luag whispered with his hand on Roland's wrist, "and I know from speaking with Katherine and her friends that your contact with me will bring me back anyway. So I will be there with you, like it or not. And Katherine has changed her mind and wishes to go as well. That's not so critical. However, if you make me disappoint the lass, I will be very angry with you myself, ye ken?"

Trembling, Roland nodded that he indeed understood.

Softening a bit, Luag pointed out, "And anyway, they won't be too mad at you once you tell them you've seen the destruction of nature in so large an area and the implications for Scotland. They'll have other things to fash about."

Roland relaxed a little. "Aye, 'tis likely ye hae the right o' it. Already I can feel nature returning to me — though I canna do much about it inside this machine."

"Good," Luag said to himself loudly enough for Roland to hear.

That made even Roland chuckle a note.

"Okay, we're here!" The MacGregor announced, opening the door on Roland's side of the monstrosity. "Here you are, sir."

Roland eagerly moved to get out alone.

But Luag still had firm a firm hold on his arm. Not wishing to give the little man even the smallest opportunity to escape back to 1411 alone, he told the MacGregor, "Close that door and come on around to this other one."

Obviously unaccustomed to taking orders, the MacGregor looked to Katherine, of all people, for direction.

She gave him a smile that would have convinced a man to give up his last copper. "Go ahead and do as he says, Greg. It's all right."

With a dopey grin on his face, the MacGregor did as she asked.

Once they were all out and the monstrosity had left, Katherine turned toward the top of the mountain and indicated a trail surrounded by the tallest pine trees Luag had seen yet.

Roland stared at the trees all the way up to the top of the trail. Several times he tried to break away toward one tree or another, and he would have forgotten to drink water if Luag hadn't insisted. Even this high up it was quite warm here, and they emptied all the little water bottles Katherine produced from her new knapsack.

When they crested the small mountain, Katherine stopped and threw up her hands with a smile. "We're here. This is as far away from civilization as I can get you in a few hours without flying."

Flying?

But Luag didn't voice his question. Roland was distracted enough by the trees. With Luag's hand still firmly on his arm, he was now leaning against the tallest one nearby, eyes closed with a look of amazement and elation on his face.

Katherine noticed. "How long do you want to give the tree hugger before we insist he take you home?"

Luag shrugged. "We can give him a few moments."

They stood there watching Roland's face move as

if he were talking to someone in his mind, which they supposed he was.

But after a while Luag grew impatient once more. "Come on, old man. We need to get home and warn our friends, and you need to get home and warn your fellow druids about all the monstrosities world domination creates, remember?"

Roland opened his eyes looking so happy, Luag was glad he'd given the druid those few moments. "If ye are ready, I think I hae just enough power tae dae the job now."

Luag opened his mouth to tell the man to get on with it.

But the world was already spinning.

In a panic, he reached out his hand toward Katherine.

She was instantly in his embrace, latching onto him for all she was worth.

Luag allowed himself to enjoy the nearness of her while the world flip-flopped all around them.

🐚

THEY ARRIVED AT THE TOP OF THE MOUNTAIN above Leif's manor. It was midday, just as it had been at the top of the mountain in Big Bear, California. And it was still July, because Luag was only slightly shivering in the skimpy clothes Katherine had purchased for him. He chuckled to see her teeth chattering as she hugged herself for warmth, goose flesh on her arms, she was so cold.

Luag let go of Roland.

The old druid ambled his way down the opposite side of the mountain from Inverurie. "Ye hae the right o' it. I dae need tae get back tae my druid kindred and show them my memories o' the terror that waurld domination brings upon nature in the future." He turned a mischievous look on Luag. "And ye need tae go and warn yer friends about yer kinsman."

Luag started down Leif's side of the mountain, wondering if Katherine would follow him.

She did, and for a time there was blessed silence between them, silence being golden during times of tension between allies, so far as Luag was concerned.

When at last she did speak, it was not with the anger he'd been preparing himself for. No, her voice was sickly sweet in the Gaelic the druid magic formed her words into.

"Sae Donald is kin tae ye?"

At first, he was at a loss as to how to respond. "Aye" was all he said, keeping his eyes on the faint trail down the mountain toward Leif's manor.

"And I assume ye want me tae keep this little

secret o' yers safe from Leif and Taran and everyone in Inverurie?" she said in mockingly sweet tones.

She had crossed the line.

He rounded on her. "They all dae ken, every last one o' them. If ye had been paying attention tae anyone but yer sacred self this past year, ye would hae kenned as well. I hae had enough o' yer superior attitude. If yer gaun'ae speak tae me, dae sae with respect. Otherwise, I would rather na hear from ye."

"Suits me just fine," she said with that same superior attitude.

Well they are almost back to Cresh Manor now, so there really wasn't any need for him to speak to her anyway.

※ 6 ※

Katherine was in shock at the venomous way Luag had spoken. It certainly didn't help her believe he was on the up-and-up with her friends. The sooner she got to them and warned them about him, the sooner her heart would be at ease.

They went up over a ridge in the mountain and there it was below them, Cresh Manor.

Katherine was startled to feel affection for the place that had seemed like a prison the past year. Must be just because her friends were there, that was all. Smoke flew from both chimneys, and the smell of roast game made her mouth water.

She needed to find better places to eat at home, that was for sure, places that used fresh ingredients. She took out her phone and made a note. "Look for farm fresh eating places, and shop at the farmers' market."

She'd had three of PenUlt's top-of-the-line solar chargers delivered to their hotel suite in her new leather messenger bag. She imagined with some excitement Lauren and Jessica's faces when she gave them theirs. Oh, they wouldn't be able to call anyone or text anyone or get on the Internet, of course, but they both had books they loved on their phones, and photos of family and friends.

"Katherine," Luag said from behind her. His businesslike tone made her cautiously turn and see what he wanted. He was holding out Leif's mother's summer linen leine. He had already put his own on.

Nodding in begrudging gratitude, she accepted it from him and put it on over her mini dress, along with the handmade shoes Lauren had bought for her. Their friends in the manor house were one thing, but as the Laird over Inverurie, Leif often had visitors from among the townspeople. They would undoubtedly be shocked at seeing Katherine in less than a leine.

The two of them went down the rest of the way in silence, with Katherine's anxiety only slightly relieved by the kindness he'd just shown.

Their friends ran out of the manor house and up the hill, huge smiles on their faces and yelling out greetings which Katherine could hear but not discern from this distance. Still, they warmed her heart. After what seemed like months but in reality had only been two days, she was reunited with the people who had been like family to her this past year.

Jessica and Lauren both crushed her in bear hugs.

"We were sae worried aboot ye!" Squealed Jessica.

"I was na," Lauren said wryly against Katherine's back, still hugging her tight. "Did ye get any action with Luag yet?"

Katherine froze, the joy of the reunion ruined in the light of what she had to reveal. "Aboot Luag," she whispered so that only the two women who had become like sisters could hear. "He says ye ken that he's kin tae the MacDonalds who kidnapped ye, Lauren." Clinging to her friends in love, Katherine waited for the brouhaha.

But it didn't come.

"Aye," Jessica whispered back with breathless haste. "We ken. Leif does tae, and Taran, and all the toon. Luag's been here for years. He's Leif and Taran's childhood friend. They trust him like a brother, just like I trust ye and Lauren."

As Leif's wife of less than a year, Jessica was the lady of Inverurie, and it was admirable how well a formerly timid woman was adapting to the role. Nevertheless, Jessica was a nurse, a nurturer — in other words, far too trusting for her own good.

Katherine pulled back a bit so she could give their less emotional engineer friend Lauren her carefully practiced raised eyebrow, her best 'Is this true?' look.

Giving Jessica a reassuring squeeze, Lauren nodded solemnly. Then she turned her eyes back to Katherine, and they were unbelievably full of joy. She opened her mouth to speak.

But gasping with excitement for her friend, Katherine beat her to it. "I missed the wedding, did na I?"

Lauren's smile turned even more joyful if that was possible and she hugged Katherine again. "Aye, ye did, and I dinna gin tae fash, I'm sae happy!"

Katherine reluctantly let her friends go. The two of them were sisters now in reality, through marriage. It made her feel left out of something she hadn't even known she wanted.

Luag strapped the sword Leif reverently handed him to its usual place on his back and was speaking to his friend in hushed tones.

Katherine went ahead and told her friends what was going on, too. "Roland, Donald's druid, followed us back tae Santa Monica—"

But Lauren had amazing news for Katherine. "Galdus telt me. I'm rid o' him, Katherine! I stabbed him intae that fool hippie Sky Blue. They're both gone with nary a trace, and I dinna care where. I'm rid o' Galdus!"

Katherine tried to make her face a happy one. "That's wonderful, Lauren."

Lauren saw through her. "Ye're wondering what Galdus telt me about Donald's druid. Just that he is in truth a friend o' Galdus more than o' the other druids here. Which means Roland is ancient, Katherine, because Galdus is ancient."

Katherine managed a true smile, finally. "That's good. That's really good. There's hope then, because Roland saw the horrors — in his words — o' what waurld domination does tae nature. He couldna use any o' his powers, ancient or otherwise, while he was in the city. He's determined tae stop the druids o' this time from helping the MacDonalds dominate Scotland."

Jessica held up her hand and waved it around in front of Katherine's face. "Hold on. Did ye say waurld domination?"

Katherine nodded vigorously. "Aye, the druids o' this time think that somehow dominating Scotland will make them dominate the waurld. That's why they brought all those people back in time from the future, tae help them ken which strings tae pull."

Jessica looked worried. "And Galdus's druid friend Roland is gaun'ae convince the MacDonalds na tae dae that anymair, na tae try and take ower Scotland?"

Katherine shook her head. "No. No, and because Luag and I lured Donald's druid away, he's likely still hopping mad. Roland does na think he wull quit. He says the next target was Aberdeen."

Jessica called out to her husband, "Leif, Donald's after Aberdeen next. We hae tae warn the Regent!"

They didn't even stay at Cresh Manor long enough to have a meal. The men ran inside for their soldiering bags, and then, surprising everyone, they gestured for the women to follow them down to the tavern where the horses were.

Katherine, Lauren, and Jessica didn't waste any time running along, but Katherine thought Jessica was going to jinx it when she spoke her ruminations out loud.

"Leif, I am na complaining, but I'm really surprised ye are taking us along."

Leif smiled at her affectionately as they ran down the hill toward the barley fields. "Luag has convinced me that the devices the three o' ye hae may help us. We dinna ken how tae use them, but he thinks they might convince the regent o' the danger."

Katherine glanced over at the man she'd been sure only minutes ago was a traitor.

There was nothing on his face but concentration, determination, and loyalty to his friends.

"I'm sorry I doubted ye, Luag. Will ye forgive me?" she huffed out as they finished passing through the barley fields. A year ago she would not have been able to run this far this fast. It was amazing what truly roughing it could do for one's stamina.

All he gave her in return was a nod.

But it was enough. She no longer felt awful, and now she could enjoy the company of her friends for a time before she left them for good. This life just wasn't for her. She'd known that as soon as she'd taken her first sip of espresso martini. She liked the finer things in life, and while those things might exist in this time, they were reserved for the richest of the rich — royalty, not a mere lord's friends.

They ran into the tavern — a one-room establishment below two bedrooms that were seldom let out to strangers.

Leif called out to the proprietor, "We wull be taking all six horses, Gil. Luag has just returned with dire news. Donald is marching on Aberdeen. We need tae warn them. Come with the rest o' the militia on foot behind us."

Gil and both of his sons ran out to the stable and helped the men get the horses ready.

Katherine was glad she'd been here a year and knew how to ride. This ride to Aberdeen would go well, unlike the embarrassing incidents she experienced when she first got here.

7

As soon as Luag saw Katherine tacking up Golden Foot in the stable, memory kicked in, so vivid it was like yesterday instead of most of a year hence. He got Steam's tack and went about preparing his own horse for the ride to Aberdeen while the memory played in his mind like one of those TV shows.

Shortly after Leif and Jessica's wedding, they had all been in this tavern. Leif had been up to some fun.

"LUAG," SAID LEIF WITH A MISCHIEVOUS SMILE on his face, "show Katherine how tae get on Golden Foot."

With a knowing look at Leif, Luag drained his tankard of ale and got up to leave the inn, not even looking to see if Katherine would follow. "The things we dae for the love o' oor friends," he said casually, but on the word 'friends,' he stared Leif down until the man laughed.

Luag smirked at Katherine when he found her standing outside the stable with her arms crossed, waiting for him to come and protect her on her way into the stable, of all places.

Katherine had made quite a name for herself in town as the one person who could match Luag in a battle of wits, and Luag wasn't going to waste this opportunity to get some revenge on her for that.

As loudly as he reasonably could, he called her out for her cowardice of horses. "Ye canna take the heat, and sae ye are staying out o' the kitchen. Wise, that is."

Her eyes grew intense with anger. "I merely wait for the help I was promised, is all."

He puffed up his chest to emphasize he was her help, lifting his chin in a proud way that made the onlookers laugh.

She moved her chin from side to side and crossed her arms, playing the impatient master waiting for her servant to comply.

He couldn't allow her to think of him that way.

"Are ye certain ye dinna want tae go in and tell Leif ye would rather na learn tae ride? Being a lass and all, there is na shame."

Seeing a small crowd gather, a pleasing red hue came to Katherine's cheeks.

Luag felt the rush of victory.

However, she recovered enough to riposte. "'Tis ye Leif put tae the task o' seeing that I could ride, na I. Sae any shame at the incompletion o' the task will be on ye, is it na sae?"

This froze him in his tracks, for she was right. He wasn't going to admit so to her, though.

But Aiden filled in for him. "She has the right o' it, Luag. Ye had best complete the tasks set for ye by yer laird, or risk his wrath."

Leif never reacted with wrath. Even though he had only recently inherited the responsibilities of lairdship at the young age of twenty-three, he was like a loving father to his people, far more likely to show disappointment when you didn't do your duty, and so everyone laughed at this.

Katherine laughed the loudest, and she stood up straighter now, even crossing her arms and raising her chin in direct challenge.

He had made this into a battle of wills between them. She would resist learning to ride and put all the blame on him!

LUAG LOOKED OVER AT THE LASS, ADMIRING THE ease with which she now threw Golden Foot's saddle over him, holding his reins to the side as if she'd been around horses her whole life.

As he passed by on his way to the tack room, he gave her his best apologetic look. "Katherine, ye were right tae ask that promise o' me. I had na idea just how wrong I was tae take lightly yer discomfort with the ways o' my time. 'Tis I who need tae ask yer forgiveness."

That pleasing redness came to her face again, and no doubt she was remembering how he'd taken his revenge on her for that victory there in the town.

LUAG GOT UP ON GOLDEN FOOT HIMSELF AND handed her up behind him, ignoring the feel of her front pressing against his back, gripping her legs around his, and the thrill that went up his spine at the feeling of her arms around his waist.

"Saddle up Steam for me," he said to Gil's younger son.

Leading the other horse behind them, he went off down the trail toward Aberdeen half an hour before stopping to give Katherine instruction in private, where no audience would give her the satisfaction of holding his obligation to teach her over his head. No, here it would just be her embarrassment and his superior skill. Just the way he liked it.

And she knew his intention, because her grip around his waist got tighter with every passing mile.

With great joy in what he was about to experience, he quickly dismounted and stepped away from Golden Foot.

"Verra well. Yer foremaist lesson will be dismounting on yer own. Ye need tae be able tae dae this with nary any men handing ye doon, ye ken, as the safety o' yer life demands it. What is yer foremaist idea about how tae proceed?" Knowing she had absolutely no idea what to do, he stayed there imitating a calm wait for her answer, drumming his fingers on his crossed arm and smiling at her with mock patience and friendliness.

She made several attempts at an answer, but each time she thought better of what she'd been about to say. Instead, she sat the horse quietly for a good quarter hour, refusing to ask for help.

Giving Golden Foot credit, he behaved remarkably well during this time, only eating the weeds he could reach without taking a step.

When Luag saw that the horse had run out of

weeds to eat, he patted Golden Foot's back, cooing, "There's a good lad. How ye can stand for the likes o' this lass I will never ken, but a good job ye are doing."

He led the horse a few steps away, where there was a large clump of grass. Only for the happiness of the horse did he do this, mind. It was no skin off his nose if Katherine was surprised and fell off his back. She was a thorn in his side. Had been from day one, and he would like nothing more than for her to learn a lesson the hard way.

No, he moved the horse for the horse's good.

Katherine was so stubborn, she sat on that horse for an hour, patiently allowing Luag to keep moving it to new clumps of grass rather than ask to be shown how to get down off the horse's back.

But Katherine had drunk several tankards of ale in the tavern.

The first telltale sign was the ever-so-pleasing red tone that came into her milky white face.

The second was a very brief grimace, before she covered it with her usual mask of self-control and contentment.

And third was the cunning that showed on her face briefly while she thought of a way to ask for what she wanted without seeming to do so —a skill of hers that he begrudgingly admired, so good was she.

"The grass is thicker over there across the water," she said from atop the horse, "and unlike yer boots, my shoes canna take being wet." As if she were doing him a favor, she reached out her hand for him to help her down as he usually would any lass who asked it of him.

As if he wouldn't even realize what she was up to.

But he wasn't having it. "Sae ye wish tae get doon, then?"

She huffed. "Ye ken I dae."

"Well then?"

"Well then what?"

"Well then, ask me nicely tae show ye."

She gritted her teeth.

He chuckled.

Growling, she relented. "Will ye please show me how tae get doon off this horse."

It was a statement rather than a question, but he would take it.

৯৯

LUAG FELT RED COLORING HIS OWN CHEEKS AT how cruel he'd been to her compared to how kind she'd been to him in her time.

Katherine saw it and rode Golden Foot over.

He searched for a way to change the subject as he got on Steam.

But with genuine kindness in her face, she told him, "I forgive ye, Luag. Thank ye for teaching me tae ride. I mean it."

He didn't want her to look away, so he said the first thing that came to his mind. "I did ye a favor that day, ye ken."

She raised an eyebrow. "Aye? Pray tell."

"Aye," he said with his best mock-superior face. "The best way tae dae some aught difficult is as fast as ye can."

8

Once more, she was on the trail to Aberdeen with Luag, and she got a bit of embarrassment when they'd been on the trail a few hours and she needed to find a bush. Thankfully, Jessica signaled to Leif that she needed one as well, saving Katherine the trouble.

Knowing how to dismount by herself now and being extremely proud of the fact, Katherine did so. After handing the reins to Luag to hold while she did her business, she ran over to Jessica and Lauren, happy to have some time alone with her friends.

But Taran handed his and Lauren's reigns to Leif, indicating he would escort Lauren.

Katherine confronted Taran. "If ye take Lauren, then who will take me? Lauren can protect me and

Jessica, sae the lasses should be able tae go off by ourselves, right Lauren? Jessica?"

Jessica shook her head no where she stood by Leif, obviously planning on helping him hold Lauren and Taran's horses.

"Lauren?" Katherine asked, knowing there was desperation in her voice but not caring. She was not going to pee within sight of any of the men.

Lauren gave Katherine an apologetic smile, holding onto her new husband as if it were the most pleasurable thing in the world to do —which Katherine allowed that maybe it was, but that was beside the point. "I'm a ninny when it comes tae fighting. Did I seem sae tough tae ye back at PenUlt? Nay. All that fighting skill was Galdus. He knew how tae fight like nay one's business, and like a fool, I let him lead me. He used his fighting knowledge tae lure me intae allowing him tae start controlling me. Now that I am finally rid o' the auld druid in that dagger, I'm as helpless as ye are. 'Tis glad o' it I am."

"May I tag along with ye?" Katherine called out after Lauren and Taran.

But they ignored her.

Having a sneaking suspicion what was going on here, Katherine turned her attention to Leif. "I dinna suppose ye wull let me tag along when ye escort Jessica tae use the bushes?"

Leif started to shake his head no.

But his wife elbowed him in the ribs, smiling sweetly while she did so.

Chuckling, Leif said, "Verra wull. Ye can tag along with Jessica. For now."

Katherine looked around for Luag's reaction to all this.

But his face was hidden. The man was sensibly doing his own business behind his and her horses while she haggled with the others.

Seeing her opportunity, she went behind the horses, feeling a strange affinity with Luag as he circled the horses around to give her privacy.

So this was how it was going to be? She and Luag were a default couple? She could work with that. It wasn't going to be how the others intended. She was not going to stay here any longer than it took to get this business with the MacDonalds sorted out short-term. Long-term, they were on their own.

When the group sighted Aberdeen, Katherine was impressed despite herself. It was a fairly large city, and even outside the gates there were hundreds of buildings.

When Taran and Lauren arrived at the gate in front of the group, the guard halted them.

"Taran, ye deserted yer men when they needed ye the night afore the last battle. Leif covered for ye, but I dinna think ye'll find a verra warm 'wull coome' inside here. Ye can bide the night at one o' the inns oot there."

Hearing this, Luag turned his horse around.

"What are you doing?" Katherine asked him.

"If Taran is getting such a poor reception, I wull dae even worse. They all ken what family I belong tae."

"We need tae go inside," she urged him.

"That's true, but we wull hae tae devise some sort o' scheme sae we are na recognized. We need an inn for tonight. Leif will hae tae hire it for us. I will hae tae sneak in like an ootlaw."

A party of English-speaking people walked by the front gate on the road. Katherine was fascinated, because everyone else was speaking Gaelic. Once they had passed by, she was overcome with anger and stormed up to the front gate and gave that guard a piece of her mind.

"Taran fought in the battle the next day, even after having tae gae all by himself ower tae Laird Ualraig's castle and rescue Lauren. If anything, I think he should be lauded, but especially na given such grief when he is just trying tae enter the city!"

The guards chewed on that a moment.

Meanwhile, a lady in the party of English-speaking people turned and winked at Katherine approvingly.

The guards were still chewing over their decision.

Katherine said to them, "Who is that lady?"

"The Lady of Bath from England," said the lead guard, who then turned to Taran. "Ye did well for yerself in the battle. Come on in."

Katherine turned to smile at her friends in triumph.

But Leif frowned at her and shook his head no, subtly signing, "Luag canna go in any case."

Oh yeah.

Katherine turned back to the guards. "I guess we wull bide ootside the city after all. Thanks anyway." She gave them her level ten smile.

It worked. They elbowed each other, grinning.

When Katherine turned around, she saw that her friends were already quite a ways down the road, apparently more desperate than she had realized not to have Luag recognized, now that Taran had been given trouble. She ran to catch up.

The problem arose again when they got to the inn. The couples wanted privacy, and Luag couldn't get a room at all.

"Loan me yer arisade," Katherine said to Lauren.

"What for?"

"Just hand it over," Katherine said with her best urgent face.

It worked.

"Here," Katherine said, putting Lauren's long, billowing plaid covering over Luag's head and pulling it over his body as if he were an old woman. "Ye are my aging mither."

Before she could instruct Luag on how to look like her aging mother, he stooped over and walked haltingly, saying in a high pitched and scratchy voice, "Ye wull take care o' getting the room, wull na ye, dear?"

Everyone laughed.

But when they got to the inn, the stable boy ran to help Katherine's 'mither' up the steps.

So Luag would be sleeping in Katherine's room with her, but she'd worry about that later. For now, they were all in Leif and Jessica's room, planning what to do.

Lauren suggested, "Leif is a laird, sae the rest o' us can enter Aberdeen as his and Jessica's servants."

The others agreed with that.

But Luag spoke up, looking them all in the eye by turns. "I hae some aught that wull guarantee I get an audience with the Regent, but not in peasant clothes. Ye wull hae tae trust me on this."

Instead of puzzlement, Leif gave Luag a knowing nod.

Katherine looked over at Jessica to see if she would reveal anything.

But Jessica shook her head no.

"Verra wull," Katherine said to the group, "sae Luag needs tae get an audience with the Regent but canna be noticed in toon. He wull hae tae go in disguise. And the best way tae accomplish that is for Luag and I tae pose as a laird and lady from England. They will na be known verra much around here, and the English are backing the Laird Regent—"

"What?"

"The English are backing the Laird Regent?"

"Ye canna mean it!"

Katherine got out her phone and brought up the book she'd downloaded, the one about the history of Inverurie. "Sorry, I thought ye all kenned that. Hear it for yerself."

9

Y e must hae it backward, Katherine," Luag said with as much gentleness as he could manage, which wasn't much. He didn't understand why, but he sat there on the floor of Leif's inn room praying it would be enough.

Good, she responded with a raised eyebrow, curiosity rather than her usual glorious haughtiness.

He explained frankly. "It would na surprise me one bit if my kinsmen the MacDonalds hae enlisted the help o' the English tae take ower Scotland, but there is na way the Stewarts would dae sae. As the rightful but incarcerated king and his regent, James and his uncle Robert already hae Scotland. If history says the English were involved, then this whole situation is more dire than I thought. 'Tis urgent, even now that Roland will dissuade the druids."

This brought the mood down. Jessica laid her head on Leif's shoulder, where the two sat side by side on the bed. Taran slumped where he stood against the door holding Lauren.

Leif gave everyone a pointed look. "That is enough talk for this evening. Let us recommence on the morrow."

Katherine raised her face with resolution, however. "I think just Luag and I should gae in and talk tae the Regent."

A change in the set of Leif's jaw told Luag his friend was about to nix this idea.

But Katherine raised her hands and quickly signed for him to please give her a chance to finish.

Leif relented, telling her so with a quick raise of his head.

After briefly looking surprised, she rushed into her sales talk, which she had plainly thought through in great detail. "We already had trouble with Taran going in, and everyone kens ye are his brother, Leif. Aye, ye hae explained everyone kens Luag is a MacDonald, but he could enter Aberdeen as my aged mither. Just two women with marketing baskets on their arms should raise na fashing."

Leif shook his head no. "Ye made quite a name for yerself last evening. Ye as wull are memorable now."

But she didn't give up. "Then I wull put Jessica's plaid ower my head and we wull both be auld women."

She looked at Jessica for her approval.

Jessica nodded that of course that was fine with her, but she raised her own objections. "Yer charm will na work nearly sae wull as an auld woman, and certies ye canna expect two auld peasant women wull be admitted intae the Regent's presence?"

"Ye hae the right o' it," Katherine said, seeming to accept defeat for a moment.

But then she spoke up again with that scheming gleam in her eye which drew him to her like a moth to a flame. "'Tis why we wull gae tae the Lady o' Bath. We wull gae at first light through a different gate and ask the guard where she bides. She winked at me last night, impressed by my bluff. Luag wull reveal himself tae her as a MacDonald, once she invites us in. If the MacDonalds and the English are in on the invasion together, then she wull be happy tae help us any way she can."

Luag nodded slowly as the cleverness of her plan sank in. "But I hae tae warn the Regent aboot the impending attack. She will na take ower wull tae that."

Katherine smiled indulgently at him, the way one smiles at a small child who has stated something obvious. From a man it would've infuriated him, but somehow from her it made him like her.

When she spoke, the feeling intensified.

"O' course. But Luag wull insist on speaking with the Regent privately."

Luag looked to Leif. "'Tis a good plan. I agree. The rest o' ye bide here at the inn and we wull rejoin ye in at most tae days. If we have na come oot in tae days, then try some other way o' getting the news tae the Regent."

Leif nodded sagely and then looked to his wife as if for comfort, but in in truth this was his way of signaling the others it was time to leave.

So they did. Taran and Lauren quickly went to their own room and closed the door before Luag could ask Taran if he could sleep in there and Lauren could sleep in Katherine's room.

Nope.

Luag turned to Katherine.

Katherine shrugged in a pretty way, signing, "We will just hae tae bear it, I suppose. She giggled then, the sort of anxious giggle a young lass gives her lass friends when a lad smiles at her.

He smiled at her in gratitude and stepped aside, clearing the way for her to precede him into her room, the only other room here at the inn.

She opened the door and stepped inside, turning

at the last moment and holding the door open in invitation.

He accepted.

There was only one bed, a double.

"Ye take the bed," he told her even as he was taking off his weapons and stowing them beneath it within easy reach of the floor where he would be sleeping.

"That's nice o' ye, considering this is my room," she quipped, dropping her plaid on the floor for him and then scrambling under the covers fully clothed.

He piled his plaid on top of hers to make as comfy a billet as he could. "If ye need the chamber pot in the middle o' the night, just kick me and I'll roll ower tae let ye by."

She rolled over in the bed so that she was on her side, facing him. "Thank ye for permission. 'Twas my plan."

Her face was so smug, he wanted to pinch it. He settled for a mock pinch in the air in front of her nose. "Sae ye are na longer angry with me ower being a MacDonald?"

"That was na why I was angry."

"Oh?"

"Nay. I was angry because I thought ye had kept it a secret. Ye canna help what clan ye were born intae."

He couldn't help the smile on his face as he drifted off to sleep. The room was dark. Mayhap she wouldn't see.

10

K atherine and Luag inquired of the guards at the other gate where the Lady of Bath was staying and then made their way to her townhouse.

An English girl answered the door. "Prithee pardon me. Milady has asked me to turn away all beggars. 'Tis nothing personal, thou must needs understand—"

Before the girl could conclude and shut the door, Katherine revealed her young face and showed the girl the ring on her finger, the expensive old-fashioned ring she'd bought on Santa Monica's 2nd Street Promenade. Had it been just two days ago?

"We are na beggars," she told the servant, "And we think yer lady has good reason tae speak with us."

The girl stared back and forth from the ring to Katherine's face. "I remember you."

Now she smiled at Katherine in admiration. "You are the Scottish lady who talked her way into the gate yesterday. You're right. Milady was impressed with you." She opened the door all the way and gestured inside. "Please come in and have a seat, and I will go tell her you have arrived."

The sitting room looked surprisingly similar to many living rooms Katherine had seen in modern life. It didn't have a TV, stereo, or anything electronic at all of course, but many of her friends' parents liked their living rooms to be just so, places where you talk to your guests rather than places of entertainment for the family. There were comfy chairs and end tables and knickknacks. There was even a grandfather clock.

A few moments later, the girl returned.

Two other girls came close behind her, fussing over the Lady of Bath, who was older, probably in her 50s, and had to be helped down the stairs.

Arthritis, Katherine thought.

The lady beamed a smile at Katherine. "Martha tells me you're quite well to do, but also that you request my assistance. I was quite impressed with you yesterday at the gate, and I'm intrigued. Please tell me the nature of the help you request."

Katherine looked around at Martha and the other two girls.

The lady shook her head no. "I'm impressed, but I cannot extend too much trust, you understand."

Luag tapped Katherine's shoulder.

She turned to give him an irritated retort.

But she was brought up short by what she saw. Four armed men stood close at hand in the hallway.

The lady gave Katherine a genuine smile. "Anything you're going to say to me, all my people can hear. They were born into my service, and they're loyal. I trust them with my very life, as you can see, and so does my husband, who is gone to court for the day as usual."

Luag spoke up now, mostly addressing the warriors. "We request yer assistance in getting me tae court. I wish tae speak with the Laird Regent about this matter o' his resistance tae Donald Laird o' the Isles' claim on the region o' Ross. If I can get an audience with him, things will gae more smoothly for everyone, with less bloodshed. For I am a MacDonald, ye see."

The lady narrowed her eyes at Luag, measuring him up. "How do you think I can get you in?"

Katherine piped up. "Perhaps we could be yer children?"

They wrangled over it an hour, going over all the

possible problems, but the lady kept looking at Luag with keen interest, and in the end she agreed.

"It just so happens we have some English clothes that might be made to fit you on short notice." She eyed Katherine's ring. "Of course, such clothing is expensive."

Katherine took the ring off and held it up, giving Luag an 'I told you so' look and signing, 'Who are you to tell me what not to buy.' Out loud, she said to the lady, "Once we have the clothing, you may hold this ring as surety for it."

❦

Luag walked through town next to the lady's litter with his head covered —ostensibly against the chill, this time. They swept right into the Regent's Aberdeen residence, a sizable manor house. Once inside and out of earshot from the street where a mob might be assembled, he uncovered his head, interested to see who among all these lesser nobles present would recognize him —and still more interested to hear who would call him out for his presence.

He found out quickly.

"My, my, my, isna that the MacDonald who

attempted tae stop us from defending oorselves at the recent battle?"

"Bide a bit," said Luag. "If I could stop ye from defending yerself, then ye are na much o' a warrior, are ye?" He looked up into the buffoon's face and held the man's gaze until he looked away.

Satisfied, Luag then proceeded down the hall, where he had several more such exchanges, winning every last one. It was is all well and good for these nobles to hang back behind their clansmen and let others do their dirty work. That was their prerogative, but Luag was the sort who did his own fighting, and everyone knew it. Most respected it. Those who didn't at least feared it, and that gave him a self-satisfied grin.

HE SPENT SO MUCH TIME PAUSING AND TALKING that the Lady of Bath caught up to him. "You certainly do run off a lot for a man who wants me to make an introduction," she said with mock irritation. "I almost think that wasn't your intention at all." Here, she looked him in the eye and raised her eyebrows, inviting him to confess the true nature of his visit to the Regent.

He couldn't do that, and so he held out his arm for her.

With a playfully superior look toward Katherine, the lady took his arm. "Come. I found out where the Regent is. I'll take you to him straightaway."

Dutifully, Luag slowed down to the auld lady's pace, resisting the urge to turn and see what Katherine thought of this.

He could hear Katherine following them, so she couldn't be in too bad of spirits over it. Why he cared was beyond him, but he found that he did. Couldn't let it trouble him though. He needed his wits about him.

The lady gestured to the double doors they wanted, smiling at the two guards.

They smiled back and opened them for her, one of the them announcing, "the Lady of Bath."

Even in the Regent's inner sanctuary, an ordinary sitting room not unlike where Katherine and Luag and waited for the Lady of Bath, a dozen people doted on him.

The Regent took note of their entry and visibly excused himself from the small crowd of people gathered around him in order to look up at the lady. "My dear, welcome. Ye are early. Yer husband said ye would na be coming till supper, but yer presence is welcome now nonetheless."

The Lord of Bath excused himself and came over to take over escorting his wife.

Before he got there, she spoke up, curtsying. "Robert, I bring you Luag MacDonald, nephew to Donald MacDonald. He has news for you that he thinks will help solve the conflict with Donald, using less bloodshed. I know it was rash of me to bring him."

Everyone in the room gasped.

"Ye dare bring a MacDonald in here?"

"He and whoever came with him must be thrown out straight away."

"They retreated, and now they send one warrior tae negotiate?"

The Regent opened his mouth to speak and was gesturing toward the guards.

Luag took a big breath and as quickly as he could, said what he'd come to say. "Donald is na gaun'ae stop at that one battle. Even now, he marches on Aberdeen. Ye need tae prepare and meet him, or I fear ye will lose everything."

The guards grabbed him and Katherine and were carrying them out.

The Lord Regent was saying, "They may stay in Aberdeen for now, but get them oot o' my house."

Before the door closed and the Regent couldn't hear him, Luag managed to call out, "The English are with Donald. They are working together. They already hae James captive, and now they want ye. Be on yer guard!"

The doors closed with a final bang.

Katherine and Luag were taken to the front gate and summarily dumped into the street.

Luag held his hand out to help Katherine up.

But Katherine pushed it away and pushed herself up off the ground. "What dae ye call that?" She asked, her face all twisted up in anger. "Ye always take ower, talking at the most inopportune moments. I had a plan for selling the Regent on oor situation. He would hae listened tae me. I'm way more charming than ye are, in case ye hadna noticed. And then ye went and ruined it. Ye are tae stubborn and full o' yerself for yer own good, dae ye ken? Has na anyone ever telt ye that?"

Luag waited for a pause in her blathering before he said anything. He knew from experience with such matters that she would have to stop for breath. "I got said what needed tae be said," he told her. "As for letting ye sell it, ye are a lass, and a stranger at that. Ye didna hae a chance o' being heard in there. 'Tis different at home in Inverurie where everybody knows ye are under my protection —er, and Leif's protection, and Taran's. Leif is the laird there, a big fish in a much smaller pond. Here, 'tis far better I said it. I warned him. If ye had spoken up in yer usual shrewish manner, we would hae been thrown oot much sooner, dinna ye ken?"

She gave him a much sterner face. "I only came back tae this forsaken place tae help Jessica and Lauren. Ye will let me help them. I will be gone soon enough, and then ye willna hae tae fash about me anymair."

He put his foot down. "Helping yer friends ye may be, but ye must understand that I am gaun'ae help my friends. Leif and Taran are my friends, and dinna ye forget it."

They were out in the middle of the street where they had been tossed, and the yelling had drawn a small crowd. It was not the kind of crowd Luag wanted to draw, so he started walking toward yet a third gate, hoping they could make their exit without too much of a scene.

But even as he walked, she wasn't catching on. "What is this aboot ye being the nephew o' Donald Laird o' the Isles? I mean, I kenned ye were kin tae him, but his nephew? How dae I ken I can trust ye? I ken I hae asked that afore, but this makes it even more o' a question—"

A young man ran up. "Luag! Alasdair bids me take ye tae him. Quickly!"

Luag started to pull himself away from the boy, but when he looked closer, he recognized the messenger who had been with the Wolf of Badenoch's son Alasdair Stewart the night before that scene on the battlefield.

The messenger took them to a small house on the edge of town and stopped at the door to call in through the window. "Open up, Sorcha! These people need tae get off the street quickly. Please hurry!"

The door was opened by an older woman in a cook's apron, drying a tankard. "Verra well, gae on and hurry in." She gave Luag and Katherine curious looks but didn't say anything about them before going back to her bin full of dishes.

Luag took this as a good sign —not that she approved of them, but that she was loyal to Alasdair and wouldn't meddle in his affairs. That was the best that could be hoped for.

The messenger went to get his master.

In moments, Alasdair came bustling into the room with a sense of urgency about him. When he saw Luag, he stopped and put his hand on the pommel of his sword, though he didn't draw.

"Luag McDonald." He paused a moment, holding Luag's gaze with his own. "There has been much talk o' the unusual circumstances under which ye disappeared from the battlefield tae days hence. Dae ye care tae explain yourself."

It hadn't really been a question, but Luag chose to interpret it as such. "'Tis much more important we tell ye Donald Laird o' the Isles even now marches on Aberdeen. He brings with him at least as many warriors as he had back at that battlefield. Aberdeen needs tae prepare or be taken ower completely, and the Regent tae."

Alasdair raised up his other hand, keeping a firm grip on the pommel of his sword, Luag noticed. "Whoa. Ye must hae some inside knowledge o' this. Ye wull need tae tell me where this is coming from afore I wull heed, ye ken?"

The cat was already out of the bag, so there was no harm in telling one more person. Alasdair would hear it through the grapevine before the end of the day anyway. "I am Donald's nephew, is how I ken his plans." He raised his hands up in a sign of surrender and as a plea for Alasdair to keep listening to him. So far it was working. "But all that Leif telt ye is true. My loyalty is tae Leif, na tae my uncle. I truly hae come in all urgency tae warn ye o' my uncle's plans. I dinna care if ye believe anything else sae long as ye believe that ye need tae reinforce the Regent's position, lest he be also captured as James has been. For Donald is in league with the English. Ye canna trust them either. Ye need tae ken this.."

Alasdair watched Katherine's face to see her

reaction to this news, looking more and more impressed that she showed no reaction at all. In fact, this visibly turned the tide of his mind. "And ye flee now from?"

Luag lowered his eyes. "We flee now from the Regent. I telt him what I just telt ye. He did na believe me." He raised his eyes again and looked Alasdair in the face. "But now I hae hope that ye will get the message through tae him."

Alasdair sighed deeply and withdrew his hand from his sword. Now pacing the room, he gestured to some seats but didn't look to see if they sat down. "I wull dae what I can tae get the Regent on board, but that isna much, ye ken. Where are ye staying, in case I need tae get word tae ye?"

Taking hold of Katherine's hand to loop her arm through his, Luag told the man the name of their inn and then quickly escorted Katherine out of there, sensing there were things Alasdair had to do which he wouldn't do in front of them.

But Katherine resisted, giving Alasdair that winning smile of hers. "Hae ye plaids we could borrow?"

So they left in their disguises as auld women, which worked perfectly. Everyone in the crowded streets looked right through them on their walk toward yet another city gate. They would have to walk around the outside wall of the city back to their inn, but that was better than being recognized, especially at this juncture.

"I guess we are keeping the Lady o' Bath's clothes and she is keeping yer ring," Luag said to her softly with his best look of apology.

She shrugged, making her plaid dance around her. "Dinna fash on it. I thought something like this might happen, and I can afford another ring."

This heightened Luag's sense of urgency concerning her, because she could only afford such a thing in the future. She was going back. Why did this trouble him so?

"We said what we came tae say," he told her anyway. If leaving would make her happy, then leave she should.

11

Now that they had spoken to Alasdair, Katherine felt better about going home soon. Things were in motion. Luag would be fine eventually, once history was confirmed and Donald gave up trying to take over all of Scotland. That man needed to be happy with all the isles he already had under his control.

Luag was even hinting at it being time for her to go.

The idea of leaving bothered her now, though. Why? Must be her suspicion of Luag. She'd better make sure he was on the up and up before leaving Jessica and Lauren at his mercy. Yeah, that was it.

They were walking to their inn the long way, through the town that had grown up around the outside of Aberdeen's wall. Their auld woman disguises were working perfectly, and they could speak to each other in hushed tones without anyone taking notice of them.

"Sae ye are Donald's nephew."

"Aye, that I am. I canna change my parentage, ye ken."

"Trying I am, tae ken. If ye are direct kin tae Donald, why did ye leave?"

"Did na Lauren tell ye what a scoundrel my uncle is?"

"Aye, howsoever, he couldna been sae bad tae his kin. Ye must hae had it good."

Luag scoffed and was silent for a time. And then all he said was, "Ye canna imagine."

"Tell me, then," she said, not really expecting him to comply.

But he huffed out a breath and spoke. "Donald raised me tae be his protégé. All through childhood, I was his favorite. And ye hae the right o' it in a way. I never wanted for anything, growing up. I had it much better than many people." He was silent then.

She let the silence go on for a while, but patience was not her strong suit. Sooner than she knew was wise, she was asking him questions again, unable to curb her curiosity.

"Sae far, ye hae na made a verra good case for why ye left."

He laughed. It was a forced laugh, though. "This is something I dinna fancy speaking o'."

"Och, it must be verra bad. I never took ye for someone who had trouble with words."

"Wull, ye hae kenned me a year, howsoever all that time has been away from my uncle's home. He is a cruel man, Katherine. He wages war against his wife's kin. I could na stand for it. As soon as I was a warrior in my own right, I left. I roamed awhile, but then Leif's parents hired me tae train Inverurie's militia. 'Tis na secret that my people are better warriors that his, coming from Viking stock as we dae."

Despite herself, Katherine grinned a little at this last bit, raising her plaid cowl to meet his eyes even as he raised his to meet hers. "Even in my time, we revere the Vikings, so I wull give ye that."

He gave her the barest of grins back, searching her eyes.

She looked away, unwilling to hear his confession of the feelings he had for her.

They arrived at their inn just as the sun was setting over the stone buildings of Aberdeen. It had been a long walk, and Katherine sorely wished for a hot bath. Why couldn't she have one anyway? All the movies she'd seen of this time involved people hauling buckets of hot water upstairs to your room and filling a big tub so you could have a bath. One look at the people inside told her this was not accurate. They were all greasy, even the proprietor, who she thought for sure would take baths if they were available. Yeah, she was going to leave this time as soon as humanly possible.

Her friends were all eating dinner, so Katherine and Luag joined them. They couldn't say much down here in front of the locals of course. No need to embroil themselves in rumors.

As usual, the food in this time was wonderful: fresh bread, vegetables, and meat. Katherine had seconds, unsure how many more of these meals she would get to enjoy. Finding a local farmers market moved up a notch on her mental to-do list for when she got home.

So far, the Aberdeeners weren't showing any sign of realizing they were under imminent attack. The talk in the tavern below their inn was all about the upcoming grand market fair.

"Aye, and Cordy McVeigh is making her famous mutton stew again this year."

"I heard the Morris dancers were coming back, all the way from Wales."

"Aye, I heard that as wull. This year's fair should be every bit as good as last year's."

"Better, from the sound o' it."

Once they were done eating, Leif looked up toward his room.

One by one so as not to make a scene, Katherine and her friends all went to it.

Leif closed the door and the window, despite the July heat. Even then, he used their Charades sign language as much as possible, only saying words they didn't have signs for, in tones as low as could be heard by the rest of them.

"What news, Luag?"

Luag made the sign for them all being in danger before he explained what had gone on that day. "The Regent threw us oot. He says for now we can stay in Aberdeen, but that's only for now, mind. I dinna think either o' us should show oor faces in toon. Good news is before he threw us oot, I telt him aboot the impending attack. Also, Alasdair is here. We telt him as well, and unlike the Regent, Alasdair believes us. He will dae all he can, but the situation remains perilous."

Taran signed, "I can take Lauren and Jessica home and tell the militia not to come."

Jessica and Lauren both shook their heads furiously, signing "We're staying here with you."

"Send Luag also," Taran signed frantically. "He's the one who canna bide here, and I ken ye need tae bide in case ye can smooth things ower with the

Regent." He quit signing, and out loud he said, "Laird Leif."

This brought a few half-hearted chuckles.

Katherine chuckled, and she noticed Lauren did too.

Not Jessica. Jessica's eyes were proud of her husband and full of determination to protect her people.

Leif still had not answered, and so Taran frantically signed some more. "Our duty is tae Inverurie. Let Aberdeen take care o' itself. Was na sae long ago that each clan was on its own."

Leif looked like he was considering it.

Jessica moved closer to her husband, and Katherine thought she was holding his hand a little too tightly for it to be simple affection.

With a sad but determined look on his face, Leif signed, "Inverurie will na be safe if Aberdeen is taken. When the militia come, oor best course o' action is tae face the threat with as many men as we can muster. And pray this time will be the last."

Everyone but Luag nodded in agreement at this.

Luag kept to himself, plainly mulling something over. Deep thought was not in his nature, so Katherine knew something was up.

The two of them stayed and visited with their friends for a few more minutes, but the married couples were obviously anxious to be alone, so she and Luag left.

"Want tae go doon tae the tavern and hae a drink?" He asked her with a bit of an awkward grin.

She smiled up at him conspiratorially, the unspoken agreement not to be alone in their room longer than necessary lingering in the air between them. "That sounds lovely."

When they got downstairs, the day crowd had left. The tavern's evening crowd was more boisterous.

Luag's protective hand drew her arm through his so that they locked elbows, making Katherine smile despite herself. "'Tis best ye pose as my wife for propriety's sake, ye ken."

She nodded in agreement, letting him lead her over to a table near the door, where the biggest crowd had gathered around a musician playing on a mandolin. By turns, different singers took up verses of a long ballad.

Luag took a turn, showing off a beautiful tenor voice Katherine never imagined him having.

Laird Hamleton dremd in his dream,

In Caruall where he laye,

His halle were all of fyre,

His ladie slayne or daye.

Busk and bowne, my merry men all,

Even and go ye with me;

For I dremd that my haal was on fyre,

My lady slayne or daye.

Amid everyone enjoying themselves, Katherine felt bad for these people whose Regent didn't take their defense seriously. They even drank to his health. She cast a worried glance over at Luag and signed, "Will Alasdair get through tae him? Will he defend these lovely people?"

"I hope sae," he signed back before picking up his mead and sipping daintily as befitted the nephew of a laird.

Why hadn't she noticed before, his noble manners? Without thinking about it she knew they'd always been there.

They sat and passed the time that way pleasantly for a few hours until at last they tired.

12

Luag knew he was lying on the floor in Katherine's room at the inn, asleep and dreaming, but that didn't lessen the horror. He was back on Islay as a child, almost a man. Donald and the other warriors were preparing to attack his favorite cousin Angus's household. Angus was old enough to be fighting in the conflict, though Luag wasn't, not quite.

Luag ran up to Uncle Donald and pleaded with him. "Let me gae along, Uncle. I'm ready. Ye said yerself I was ready for battle."

Annoyed but trying not to show it, Donald turned to the other warriors and gave them a look that said leave us.

They all did, knowing better than to mumble among themselves about it.

Donald put his hand on Luag's shoulder. From a distance, it probably looked like a reassuring pat on the shoulder.

Luag knew otherwise. This was Donald asserting his authority over Luag by showing how much taller and broader he was. Luag's arms looked scrawny next to Donald's arms, and he knew if he challenged his uncle, he would be crushed to the ground and possibly killed.

When Donald spoke, his voice was stern. There was no pretension of sympathy or reassurance. "Ye are too soft, Luag. I ken why ye want tae go. Ye want tae warn Angus. I will na let ye. Someday, ye wull see the wisdom in this, but for now, ye wull bide home and help tae protect the lasses. I ken I hae been clear. I ken ye will obey."

As all the other warriors left for battle, Luag shed his last tears. Whether his uncle realized it or not, that conversation with him had made Luag a man. Right then and there, Luag had decided he was leaving. He would rush ahead and warn his cousin, and then he would never return to the MacDonald clan.

He told only his mother, who hugged him and cried.

With a start, Luag snapped awake. He needed to leave right away, before everyone else awakened. He would just get dressed and go. He had provisions in his soldiering bag for a ten-day trip, and they'd only been on the road for two days.

He jumped up and grabbed his bag, but it wasn't to be. Katherine wasn't in the room.

Slamming his fists against the door, Luag cursed. And then he rushed to join the others downstairs, where he could smell parritch and, now that he was paying attention, hear talk and laughter. If he couldn't get a head start, he might as well break his fast before he left.

Jessica was the first to greet him when he joined them at their table in the downstairs tavern. "Wull good morrow, sleepyhead. Katherine says ye were snoring sae loudly she didna hae the heart tae wake ye. She already prepared ye some food ta take away." She indicated a bundle in the middle of the table with a twinkle in her eye and a wrinkle in her nose, then relaxed at Leif's side.

Luag pulled the bundle of bread and cheese over to him and nodded to Katherine. "I thank ye. That was considerate." Rather than eat the store of provisions, he put them into his soldiering bag, which he had carried down with him.

Katherine noticed. "We are na leaving. I was

gaun'ae bring that up tae the room for ye when the rest o' us finished eating. But ye dinna hae tae eat that now. Hae some hot parritch. 'Tis good. Murag! Bring Luag here some parritch, please. Thank ye." She sounded like she meant it, when she said the parritch was good.

This amused Luag, given her bent for the finer things in life and parritch being such peasant fare. It was on the tip of his tongue to tease her about it.

But he didn't. If he even looked at her, this would be too difficult. She was too beautiful, and her smiles were too rewarding. And she was being too kind to him... lately. "Wull I am leaving. Just as soon as I finish breaking my fast."

Everyone put their food down.

Jessica was first to speak. "Ye dinna hae tae leave, Luag. Bide with us."

Taran spoke up next. "Aye, if anyone has a problem with ye biding, we wull show them the way."

Lauren nodded her assent. "I hae some ideas aboot ways we might defend oorselves, should the need arise."

Katherine spoke at last. "Where will ye go? And why?"

Before he could stop himself, he looked at her. It was as big a mistake as he had known it would be.

Never mind that her face was beautiful. Her eyes held concern for him, such concern as he hadn't seen since that night he left his mother fifteen years before.

Like him, Katherine had donned once more her Scottish clothing, no doubt stuffing the English outfit so dearly bought into her new leather satchel, which she had with her as always.

Spurred by her concern, he answered more completely than he had intended. "History must be preserved. It lost its way in part because o' me. I was the one Roland grabbed hold o'—"

Katherine shook her head no and rushed to say, "It wasna ye. 'Twas because I was there. I was the one he was following tae the future." Those last three words had been signed rather than spoken, but judging by the look on her face, it had been a near thing. The red embarrassed tone in her cheeks made her even lovelier.

He drank her in, knowing full well he would never see her again —oh, mayhap he would, when she came to visit Jessica or Lauren for brief periods. 'Twould make it even worse, seeing her only briefly and then having her taken away from him again. He forced his eyes away.

Meanwhile, Jessica and Lauren were signing as well. "We are the ones who traveled back in time and fed the druids' plan tae ken the future. 'Tis our kind tae blame, us time travelers, not ye."

"'Tis all my fault," signed Lauren with the saddest face ever. "I wanted tae coome back in time sae much. I hae brought Scotland tae the brink o' ruin."

Luag's parritch came, and he tore into it, using it as an excuse to gather his thoughts before he spoke this time. As he ate, he made a real effort to enjoy the food. Hot parritch was far better than the hardtack he'd be living on during his journey. Too soon, it was all gone and he had no excuse to postpone telling them. Why hadn't he woken up in time to leave while they yet slept?

Looking into the lasses' worried faces made him glum. "History must be preserved sae that Scotland remains natural and beautiful. I am na just doing this in defense o' ye lasses, ye ken."

Lauren raised up her hands in frustration. "Tell us what ye are doing, already."

Not looking at them for fear of catching something in their eyes that would take his courage away —not just Katherine's eyes, mind— Luag signed, "I am gaun'ae play the prodigal son, wull nephew. I wull return tae Uncle Donald, look at his war machine from the inside, and bring it doon." Without looking to see their reactions, he got up, grabbed his soldiering bag, and headed out to the stable.

🐚

Katherine took but one second to look into Jessica and Lauren's eyes and panic. She was reassured in what she saw from them. They both smiled their encouragement, nodding and subtly and signing, "We'll keep in touch through Kelsey's dreams."

Bolstered by their support and not caring what the men had to say, Katherine got up, put her leather backpack and plaid on, and ran out the door to catch up with Luag. He needed someone with him who was in touch with what was really going on.

She understood why Leif and Taran didn't dare go. As a laird, Leif's description at least was known all over the kingdom, if not beyond. And Taran was Leif's brother, the one who had left the practice field suspiciously. Jessica and Lauren were going to stay with their men of course. This only left Katherine to go and be Luag's connection to Kelsey and the help she had to offer. Katherine had to go.

She kept telling herself this as she watched Luag tack up his horse and mount, then ride out as himself, free from the plaid over his head to disguise him as an old woman.

True, he was going away from the gate where he had been recognized, but still.

Anger flared up in her. That man was so stubborn. Without consulting anyone, he had struck out on his own, following his own plan. When she did catch up to him, she was going to give him a piece of her mind, that was for sure.

Panic struck her, and she hurried after him. No time to tack up her own horse. She couldn't lose sight of Luag before he got too far out of the city and could go faster than a walk. He could change direction and she might never find him. But she couldn't catch up with him too soon, or he'd just turn around and march her right back to their friends.

Her legs felt the journey not at all, and she smiled, adding daily workouts of at least three hours to her lengthy 'to do' list . No sense wasting all the conditioning she'd done over the past year, albeit quite involuntarily. This was the best shape she'd ever been in, bar never. She felt awesome.

All in all, it was quite a pleasant walk, and her mind wandered a bit as she stayed close enough to keep her eyes on Luag but not so close that he would notice her following.

What was her angle, for selling these new leather backpacks? With her new physique, she could add to her repertoire being an expert at exploration in rugged places like the Highlands. This bag meant you could pack light but still have everything you needed built in, convenient and impossible to forget.

It was tempting to get her phone and take pictures of herself amid all these people, wearing her backpack — or possibly, getting one of them to take a picture! But she didn't dare. If they stole her phone, the implications were too mind numbing to consider. Still, just a selfie shot of herself on that cliff over there with the ancient city of Aberdeen in the background would give her so much credibility...

She passed several hours this way before the crowds thinned, the road opened up, and she was forced to catch up with him.

❧ 13 ❧

Finally, Luag was catching a break. There was a small river where Steam could drink, and then the road was wide open.

His luck changed, however. He had just remounted when Katherine came along. She didn't make a scene, didn't call out his name or call him husband and ask why he was deserting her.

No, she merely stood on the side of the road and gazed up into his eyes, defying him to leave her there.

He cursed.

But he reached out a hand and lifted her up to ride in front of him, even though she wore her small knapsack on her back. He would've put her behind him, except that his soldiering bag was tied there, along with provisions that had come with the horse.

She lifted her leg over Steam's neck to ride

astride, then nestled in front of him as if it were her right, curse the woman. Softly, for his ears only, she said what he'd been dreading. "I could na let ye desert me, 'Husband'."

Feeling things he ought not feel, he spoke tersely. "Where dae ye think I gae, tae a market fair? I hae enough tae dae seeing tae my own hide. Certies I dinna need ye tae look after. I wull make ye regret cooming along. Och, aye, I wull."

With that remark, he whipped the horse into a gallop that took them off the road and across a shortcut through the heather.

Her fear caused her to hold tightly to his legs on either side of her, pushing herself backward into him.

It made his mouth water, among other reactions she undoubtedly could feel.

Inwardly, he cursed his shortsightedness. He couldn't have her doing that. "If ye keep on that way, I wull insist we be marrit in truth, and then where wull ye be, hm?"

She instantly stopped herself from pressing into him, but she turned to give him a derisive look that would have made him jump off the horse if she could fight. Her spirit was what he most enjoyed about her, even more than her beauty and wit.

And then he heard his name from back on the road.

When he saw the source, he said to her, "Hold on. We hae been spotted by some o' the Regent's men, and now we really dae hae tae run."

She gripped his legs, not pressing back into him.

But the horse's run over the rough terrain jostled her so much, Luag took one hand off the reins and grabbed hold of her with his other arm, pulling her into him for all he was worth.

His words plainly on her mind, she kept stiffening against him in indignation at this and then relaxing when she forgot to be indignant. Over and over. Which made it difficult for him to concentrate on steering the horse through the trees at a run.

Steam agreeably jumped over hedges and ducked under branches, swirled around thickets and waded through a stream, all without the least complaint. Luag was proud of him.

Before Steam got too winded, they no longer heard hoofbeats behind them.

Luag dismounted and reached up to hand Katherine down.

But she turned her nose up at him and slid down on her own.

He walked Steam to let the horse cool down, then got his water skin down while letting the animal take a long drink from the river. After he had drank his fill, he held the skin out to Katherine.

But she was down on all fours, cupping water out of the river with her hand and trying to be dainty about it, but still getting quite a bit on herself.

Smirking, he rearranged the provisions a bit, got on the horse, and started it across the three-foot-deep river.

"Och, nay ye dinna," she declared, running up and grabbing hold of his trew leg. "Back up and let me mount."

He waited a beat.

She slapped his knee! "Now!"

It didn't hurt, and he stifled a laugh as she climbed up, this time behind him.

She clung to his back as the horse splashed through the water. This was pleasant. This, he could handle.

But his thoughts soon turned to less pleasant things.

"We wull hae tae avoid the road from now on," he explained to her. "The Regent's men assume I am their enemy, and Donald's men ken me a traitor. We wull hae tae avoid all notice till we can enter Donald's camp and ask for him by name. My uncle is the only one who can safeguard us. We dinna belong anywhere."

Katherine was tempted to just relax into the warm feeling of sitting behind Luag on the horse and take what he said as the given reality. After all, what did she have to gain from taking initiative here? It wasn't as if anyone was going to award her a 'top salesperson' title in this time.

But she couldn't let his defeatist attitude prevail. "Whose fault is it we dinna belong anywhere? We left a perfectly good situation with oor friends. Let's turn aroond and go back. Gaun'ae Donald's camp is the worst idea I ever heard. What dae ye think is gaun'ae happen when we get there, they all 'wull coome' ye with open arms?"

By the tightening of his muscles, she knew he disagreed and was about to be stubborn again. She wasn't disappointed.

"Whose fault is it that 'tis us in this situation and na just me, hm? Ye left a perfectly safe situation with oor friends for nay good reason whatsoever. I, however, hae a verra good reason for going. I'm the only one who can get close enough tae my uncle tae dae any damage tae his plans."

She was breathing heavy now, she was so incensed at his pig-headedness. "I am here because there has tae be someone with some sense in their head on this journey. I am yer way oot in case things gae bad. What were ye gaun'ae dae with nary me in that case, just stand there and take the heat?"

His legs tightened around the horse and sped it up, as if he wanted to throttle her but couldn't spare his hands. Fool man. "And just what are ye gaun'ae dae aboot any heat? I hae kenned ye a year and hae na ever seen ye use any fighting skills. Just what good are ye as an aide on this journey?"

"Ye really dinna ken, dae ye?"

"No, I dinna ken. Else why would I be asking ye?"

"Jessica, Lauren, and I hae been talking aboot it off and on the past six months, if na the last year, and ye hae na ever taken an interest in what was sae consuming tae us?"

Steam started to go faster again, making Katherine grab Luag's waist and hold on for dear life.

Her anger flared to a new peak. He was doing this deliberately, looking for her to realize she was at his mercy. He was going to pay for this once they were done riding for the day, that much she knew. But for now, all she could do was hold on tight and hope Steam grew tired before she fell off.

Of course, his legs were gripping the horse so tight there was little chance of that. Did the man not know he was doing so? Obviously not. What did he have to be angry about?

He was the one being a fool.

She was just trying to stop him.

Hope won out. Before she could fall to her death, Luag slowed Steam down to a walk again.

"That was a foolish display," she told him, pounding on his back for good measure. "Ye told me yerself the horse must na run unless strictly necessary. Now tell me, was that strictly necessary?"

He didn't say anything.

She smiled in victory. "Dinna tell me I hae the famous witty Luag tongue-tied."

His hands shook just the tiniest bit on the reins, clenching in and out. But still, he said nothing.

"Ye can let go o' the vice grip yer legs hae on the horse."

Instantly, his legs relaxed, and at the same time, he coughed, a dry cough that didn't have much convincing motivation behind it at all.

Her victory smile grew larger. Pity he couldn't see it.

His voice came to her resignedly, softly. "I hae always felt this way, ye ken."

What was he talking about? "What way?" He'd only known her a year, so he couldn't mean he'd felt like protecting her all this time.

His voice grew more urgent, as if letting out thoughts he'd held pent-up forever that were now flowing out over a broken dam that had been holding them back. "I hae always felt as if I did na belong, first at my uncle's house, and then even at my friends' house. There has always been the fear that I would be exiled, nay matter where I lived, ever since I can remember, really."

He'd never spoken to her so candidly. It did something to her, made her yearn for more. "How old were ye, when ye left yer uncle's house?"

He breathed in and out steadily for a few moments, not quite sighing, but breathing forcibly enough that she noticed his chest expanding, through both of their garments.

It made her think of jumping off the horse, but she didn't.

His voice was more sure now. "Uncle kenned I disagreed with his methods long afore I left his clan. I'm still na sure why he allowed me tae become a warrior under his trainers. As soon as I could achieve that, I did leave. Only now, years later, does it occur tae me how against his interest this was. Why did he allow me tae bide long enough tae learn all I did? Mayhap he cares enough for me as his nephew that he wull listen tae what I hae tae say now. I hae tae try tae save Scotland's natural beauty and avoid having oor lives filled with bloodshed and strife against those we should hold dear, oor kin."

She couldn't bring herself to apologize, but she did relax against him to show him she trusted him.

He stopped the horse. Ever so gently, he turned in the saddle, until their faces were inches apart and he was studying her mouth.

She couldn't let him kiss her. She would see him through this, but then she was going home. Grabbing the saddle, she brought up her leg between them and got off the horse.

He dismounted as well but put the horse between them so they couldn't see each other.

They walked this way in silence for a time before he spoke again, his voice genuinely puzzled and a little hurt, but not angry. "Why did ye come along then?"

She threw her arms up in the air and let them drop with a thwack against her sides. "I telt ye already. I came along tae get ye oot if things gae sour with yer uncle. Ye hae na idea what he is capable o' now, all this time after ye left. Lauren telt me some sorry things aboot him. The man is a monster, I still canna believe ye are going tae him."

Just his eyes peered over the horse's neck at her, and they were incredulous. "And I asked ye afore, what help could ye possibly be tae me on this journey?"

A snarl escaped her lips before she was able to

control herself. The man was so aggravating, so willfully ignorant.

"Lauren's druid friend, Kelsey, shook hands with me afore Lauren's druid dagger brought us here tae yer time," she told him as patiently as she could under the circumstances, "sae Kelsey is able tae bring me intae her dreams, where I can ask her tae get help. Donald's ex druid Roland was nice enough tae help us back here and all, but ye hae tae admit, Kelsey is oor best bet at escape."

She waited for him to acknowledge her offer in some way.

When it wasn't quickly forthcoming, she lost all patience. "Dinna ye ken? I am yer only hope!"

"Why would yer precious Kelsey help me?" Luag asked hotly. But there was hurt in his voice.

"Because I'm Lauren's friend, Kelsey is Lauren's friend, and ye are my friend."

"Am I really yer friend?"

"Two days ago, I would hae said no, but I hae coome all this way tae help ye, sae aye, I ken now ye are my friend."

He kicked a stick and it went skittering across the grass. "It does na matter. Even among my friends, I hae always been an ootsider. I never truly belong. Ye should na hae coome, Katherine. I will only let ye doon."

A voice came from the top of the hill beside them. "That may be, Luag, but we canna let ye run around loose sae near camp, now can we?"

Katherine looked up and saw two highlanders up on top of the hill. Even from a distance, they looked menacing. "If we get on Steam, we can get away from them," she whispered.

Luag held his hand up to stop her from getting on while he called up to the people on top of the hill. "I planned on gaun'ae yer camp anyway. Take me tae my uncle."

Gehrig, Igor, meet my wife, Katherine."

Katherine's heart pounded, but their captors didn't touch her. That might've had something to do with Luag's hand being possessively around her waist.

Gehrig took Steam and climbed on, while Igor followed her and Luag, gesturing for them to follow the horse. It had all the provisions, so obviously they were going to go along peacefully. Besides, Luag had backed away and allowed the horse to be taken.

What did these men think of their erstwhile clansman? Did they scorn him? It was impossible to tell, with their stoic exteriors.

It didn't take long at all to reach the camp. Igor tied the horse with Luag's soldiering bag up with the rest of the horses and then moved on. Katherine was glad she had her backpack. Just like PenUlt's website said, she had all the necessities right there on her person in an emergency.

"Gae and tell Donald Luag is here and wishes tae see him," Gehrig told a boy, then turned to Luag. "Ye will pardon me for not offering ye refreshment."

Apparently this was a joke, because Luag chuckled a note.

Gehrig moved his mouth the tiniest bit toward a smile.

The three of them stood there in silence amid the busy camp with people passing by, pointedly ignoring Luag. Some of them moved their mouths the slightest as Gehrig had, but no one said anything to Luag.

He took it in stride, standing there just as stoically as Gehrig was.

Katherine was glad for his hand on her waist. Because she was with 'the man who must na be greeted,' no one said anything to her, either. There were no catcalls, which were what she could normally expect when entering a camp full of strange men.

Suddenly, everyone parted ways, forming a column of people to the left and the right.

Laird Donald all but strutted down the resulting aisle, his face full of fake surprise.

She half expected a fanfare to sound.

Donald stopped a few feet short of Luag, looking Katherine over with interest that was obvious to her, but perhaps not so much to Luag, which worried her a bit.

Lauren had been at this man's mercy and had told Katherine all kinds of horrors.

This man was not to be trusted. How could Luag not see that?

At least he probably wouldn't kill her. She didn't possess what he wanted: Lauren's druid dagger. What he likely would do to her was much less pleasant to think about. She didn't want to show weakness, but she cowered away from the man nonetheless.

This got her an amused eye from the Laird o' the Isles, but the lion's share of his attention was focused on his nephew. "After ye snuck off in the night all those years ago, I did na think tae ever be graced again with yer presence, nephew."

Well, this was Luag's chance to speak. Katherine hoped he didn't waste it.

He didn't. "Uncle, after living for years in a backward toon among those whom I had tae instruct in hand-tae-hand combat, I hae seen the error o' my ways. I hae bought my wife Katherine with me back tae ye who will be king." With this, Luag bowed his head to Donald.

The Laird gave Luag a smile of thanks, but Katherine wasn't fooled one bit.

The horse was too far away for her to run. How was she going to get Luag away so he could live long enough for Kelsey to help them?

Making a show of clinging to Luag, she whispered, "I'm gaun'ae run off. While they are distracted, ye can get away."

Luag grabbed her wrist and held it as tight as the vice grip of his legs had been earlier. He was more of a fool than she thought. Barely audible even to her, he whispered, "All will be well sae long as we show faith in Donald. Ye hae tae trust me, lass."

"Ye, I trust. 'Tis yer uncle I dinna."

Donald was still smiling at Luag in thanks, slowly walking around the two of them, looking them over. Perhaps Luag saw a doting uncle checking out the amount Luag had changed over the past ten years.

Katherine saw a man sizing them up as animals and calculating how soon they would be ready for the slaughter. She didn't want to be right. Not this time.

Donald's countenance turned cold when he had circled all the way around and come face-to-face with Luag. He held his nephew's gaze a few seconds, sternly rebuking him with only his eyes before he called out to his men, "Prepare tae hang him as a traitor," and stepped back another few feet out of the way while a bunch of highlander warriors encircled them with pikes raised high and daggers pointing at them.

Katherine grabbed onto Luag as if to embrace him for the last time as her husband before his death —all so that she could whisper with her mouth right up to his ear so no one would hear. "Ye should hae let me run."

The two of them were marched to a rope which had been slung over a tree above their own horse.

The highlanders forcefully pulled Luag away from her.

She tried to hold on, but they were too strong. They put Luag on the horse right in front of his soldiering bag as if he were going to ride off to battle, but then they put the noose over his neck.

The fool man was stoic and still all the while. He didn't fight back. He didn't lift a hand against his precious clansmen, whom he was so loyal to, that the idiotic fool didn't mind being killed by them.

Letting her face show the anger she felt, she signed to him, "Ye had better not get me killed tae, or

I wull hound ye all the way tae Hell afore I gae up tae Heaven."

The barest hint of a smile showed on Luag's face just as Donald strode up to swat the horse into running out from under the hanging man, allowing him to drop and be strangled.

She had to admire it, such stoicism in the face of the ultimate danger. She didn't think such manliness existed in her time anymore, not that she had seen, not in civilization. Perhaps in the third world that still existed, but despite being the top salesperson for a survival company, she never intended to go to the third world. This year in 1410 Scotland had been more rustic charm than she'd need in her lifetime.

She was only the head salesperson because of her charisma and her business sense. She went after the CEOs of the huge retail companies that carried PenUlt's products. She worked in a skirt and heels every day, trying on the products for the charm of it but never actually having used them before now. She had coworkers who went out into the wilds of Latin America and survived without human contact for weeks. She'd had no intention of ever doing anything like that before she was tricked into coming here by the druid trapped in her friend Lauren's dagger.

Glad she had the survival backpack on, she reached into the pocket under her left armpit and put her hand around a strobe signal light equipped with a siren.

It would shock Donald out of slapping the horse and give her time to jump up behind Luag and remove the noose from his neck so the two of them could ride away on steam—

Donald stopped with his arm up in the air before she even had a chance to pull the strobe siren out. "Verra wull done, my faithful nephew. Even after ten years in the company o' those lowlanders, ye held on tae yer MacDonald heritage." He took the noose off Luag's neck and helped him down from the horse, then handed him the reins, walked him over to Katherine, and left the two of them together. "'Tis wull ye hae coome back, nephew. Gehrig will show ye tae yer tent. Food will be brought tae ye, and then please join me in my tent for war council."

Luag helped Katherine up on Steam behind him, then followed Gehrig to the tent Donald had set aside for the two of them.

Katherine leaned up against Luag's front so that she could whisper, "I dinna like this. Let us just gae."

"If ye want tae gae, ye can take the horse, but I'm staying."

"I canna take yer horse and leave ye here." She sighed. "I'm staying. I just want ye tae ken I dinna like it."

"Ye hae already made that known tae me, lass. Dinna think I wull forget."

Their camp tent was just a large plaid thrown over three low bushes. Apparently it was an honor to be awarded this much privacy, because all around her she only saw sleeping billets on the ground. In the whole camp, only a dozen such tents stood proudly.

"I suppose most o' the men dinna bring their wives with them."

"More dae on the mainland, but not as many among us island folk." Luag dismounted and held out one hand to help her down and the other to indicate she should enter the tent first.

She crawled in. All that was inside was an extra-wide billet and an earthenware jar, for which she was grateful. She heard Luag entering behind her and rolled aside to give him room on the billet.

Luag climbed on top of her and kissed her!

It felt wonderful.

But what did he think he was doing?

And then she saw that Gehrig was watching through the entrance before it closed behind Luag and understood. She had the answer to her question. As soon as the flap closed, she pushed him off her.

He went willingly, but he sat right next to her on

the billet and put his arm around her, pulling her close against him.

She let him, but she turned and gave him a look that told him he'd better have a good reason.

Their faces were inches apart, so he could whisper the tiniest bit and she heard him. "They wull come back with food, aye?"

"Aye. Sae we hae tae sit like this until then?"

"Or risk them deciding ye are na in truth my wife."

That didn't bear thinking about, so she relaxed against him, instinctively knowing tension was a giveaway for anxiety, whereas being relaxed was a sign of confidence. Confidence had won her more benefits in this world than anything else had. Even false confidence.

She whispered, "Sae are ye gaun'ae gain the confidence o' everyone at the war council and then convince them Donald's plans are na tae be followed, or what? Ye dae hae a plan?"

He whispered right next to her ear, sending shivers across her back. "I hae been thinking that ower. I will need tae work on them in private one-on-one, rather than everyone all at once in a meeting. I dinna ken if ye noticed, but Donald rules by fear, rather than by merit. There are a few key cousins who, if I can sell them on my ideas, will withdraw from his company. I feel that's the best I can dae. It will reduce his forces significantly."

"That sounds good. Last battle, they outnumbered us five tae one, from what Lauren and Jessica were saying."

"Aye, and the lowlanders hae armor and far more horses. Those advantages are na small. 'Twas a close thing at the last battle, even with all these extra forces. My argument will be that in Aberdeen, there will be even more armored knights on horses. Donald can win, but the casualties will be even more significant. How will he hold all the territory out here west, including the islands, once he has spread his forces sae thin?"

They stopped talking when someone arrived with their food.

❦ 15 ❦

Luag knew his time with Katherine was coming to an end, so he clung to her more tightly than he would have otherwise, all throughout the meal. She didn't know, of course, so their conversation was light and casual, just the way he preferred it.

Aye, he had made the right decision in not telling her he'd be sending her on by herself tomorrow. She was as brave as brave could be, but she wasn't made to be a warrior's wife. For all her business sense and scheming, she was naïve about the ways of warriors in a way that he found at the same time refreshing and terrifying, when it came to her safety. And now he had to leave her alone in their tent and go to the war council.

Far sooner than Luag would've preferred, Gehrig appeared in the tent's entrance. "They await ye."

"Gehrig."

"Aye?"

"Find someone else tae escort me. And give me yer word, as a MacDonald, ye wull bide with Katherine and keep her safe whilst I am away."

"Aye, 'twill be sae." Gehrig disappeared outside the tent.

Luag turned back to Katherine.

The look she gave him made him chuckle. Her lips were determined to tell him she didn't need anyone to guard her, but her terror of being away from his protection was written all over the rest of her face. It was precisely this dual nature of hers that made her such good company. He relaxed into his chuckle and enjoyed these last bits of communication between them, their eyes drinking each other in.

The plaid parted again, and Igor was there. "I hae come tae take ye tae the Council, Luag."

Gehrig peeked in as well. "True tae my word, I wull be oot here tae see that no one bothers yer wife."

"I trust ye will na be bored whilst I am gone, dear wife." In front of him where Igor and Gehrig couldn't see, he signed to her, "Stay in the tent, and dinna call attention tae yerself."

She gave him a reassuring look and glanced

toward the knapsack on her back. "I hae some reading that I did na quite finish, ye wull recall."

Gehrig and Igor gasped, but to their credit, they said nothing and turned to face outside.

Holding Katherine's gaze still, Luag commented to her in what he hoped was an offhand way that would pacify his kinsmen, "I would na let it get around that ye, a lass, can read. Ye may find yerself put tae work. Remember the burden it is tae hae such a rare skill for a lass."

Her face reddened, and her eyes moved all about the tent, particularly to Gehrig and Igor. "Oh no!"

He put a finger over her lips. "Dinna fash. Gehrig and Igor would na gae spreading word o' anything that might take my wife away from me."

Throat clearings could be heard from outside the tent.

"Glad I am ye hae some aught tae occupy yer time whilst I am away. I wull hurry back tae ye."

He kissed her then.

He knew he didn't need to, that his friends would never doubt his word that she was his wife.

But time was running out, and when he returned after the war council it might be awkward between them, having to spend the night together again in such close proximity. No, the time to kiss her was now.

He started softly, hugging her to him lightly. He poured in all the longing he felt, all the regret about having to say goodbye to her just as he was realizing how much she meant to him.

He was surprised and amazed to feel her response. She kissed him back eagerly, deepening the kiss and opening her mouth to him. So willing was she, the two of them might have done some aught they regretted, had Gehrig and Igor not been waiting outside.

But alas, the kiss was not even a long one.

He broke away with a sigh and stepped back from her, gave her a nod and what he hoped was a reassuring smile, and then left the tent and approached the waiting Gehrig.

"I ken it canna be exciting, the idea o' standing here guarding my wife, and so I give ye the loan o' this knife the lowlanders made." Not feeling at all sorry for the lie, he held out the Swiss Army knife.

Gehrig took it, at first with skepticism and then strong interest, which played on his face despite his best efforts to control it.

As Luag walked away with Igor, he gave Gehrig the sternest look he could manage.

Gehrig nodded at him, and it was enough.

Luag knew Gehrig would do his utmost to keep her safe.

Luag and Igor walked through the camp a ways. There was hustle and bustle, getting things ready to start the morning march toward Aberdeen. Donald's plaid was the same one he'd always used, large enough to cover a tree that sheltered a dozen clan chiefs. It sat alone atop a small hill, for privacy.

Everyone looked over at Luag when he entered.

Their objections were vehement.

"I ken he is yer nephew, but he has been away sae long."

"Certies ye dinna wish him tae bide with us whilst we plan."

"Ye said it yerself Donald, he is a traitor."

"Ye canna believe he has truly returned tae embrace his MacDonald heritage."

Donald held up his hand and received silence. "Welcome, Luag. Please, dae join us." With a gesture, he dismissed Igor.

The man's footsteps had receded and no others were heard. Donald laid out his plans for their attack on Aberdeen.

When the meeting was over, Luag got up to leave.

Donald gestured for him to stay after everyone

else had left. "I always kenned ye would return tae me one day. Nay, I am na angry ye left. Ye would na hae any spirit in ye if ye had na."

His uncle's praise hit Luag's skin and slid down it like oil, but he had to take it if he was going to stay long enough to undermine his uncle's plans from the inside.

Uncle himself escorted Luag back to his tent, followed by his usual lackeys, amid almost-stares from everyone.

Katherine might not have noticed it if she'd been along, not being accustomed to MacDonald ways, but Luag knew all the signs of a people afraid to show their true opinions. These signs were what had first alerted him in to his uncle's dissimilarity from other clan chieftains, back when he was a boy. Donald claimed the absolute control he had over his clan was what made him worthy of command, but Luag's cousin's clan had not been like this at all. Neither was Leif's clan like this. They both commanded through being revered as capable leaders, not by fear.

"I trust ye wull hae a pleasant night with yer bride," Donald said with a gleam in his eye that made Luag all the more determined to see Katherine on her way in the morning.

"And I trust ye wull with yer bride as wull," Luag said with the appropriate amount of deference.

Even though this had been an impudent thing for Luag to say, Uncle chuckled and clapped him on the back before walking off.

Luag turned to Gehrig, who had stood stoically through this whole exchange, appropriately looking the other way and pretending he couldn't hear. This wasn't out of any sense of politeness or respect, Luag knew, but out of Gehrig's desire to keep his skin on his back.

Now that Donald was walking away, Gehrig gave Luag the barest smile in greeting. "This is some knife ye hae. Ye want tae sell it?" He said this even as he held it out to Luag, obviously knowing full well that Luag would not part with it for money, it being such a remarkable thing.

"I thank ye for yer appreciation and yer offer," Luag said, accepting the knife with a smirk of a smile that said he knew how valuable a thing it was and while he appreciated the offer, there was no way he was going to accept. "I trust ye had na trouble manipulating its various parts?"

They were whispering, Gehrig understanding how Luag wouldn't want this to get around, lest he be relieved of the knife in his sleep. "Quite a remarkable thing."

"Aye, the lowlanders are nary sae primitive as we are led tae believe. They are quite capable o' going on withoot oor help."

Gehrig gave the slightest wrinkle of his nose, indicating he agreed, and walked away, giving Luag's hand the barest tap, which had to substitute for a forearm grasp in the presence of such suspicion as there was in the MacDonald camp.

Luag ducked into his tent.

Katherine put what she called her phone into her bag. She did so quickly enough that if he hadn't known what it was, he wouldn't have had any idea. So far, so good.

He removed his sword and lay down on top of it on the billet next to Katherine, placing the covers over him and her but pointedly turning his back to her, his reassurance there would be naught untoward between them.

Not that he didn't want her, but he didn't wish to ruin her for marriage in the future. To someone else. He swallowed some panic rising in his throat inexplicably.

"Sae what was said at the war counsel?" she whispered next to his head.

He whispered back over his shoulder, "Donald plans on coming up from the south and surprising Aberdeen."

"I finished the book while ye were away," she whispered tentatively. "I was just reading the pertinent parts again. There is na record o' any attack on Aberdeen. Are ye certain he wull dae it?"

"Aye. I dinna claim tae ken him overly wull, especially after being gone these ten years, but aye, he is gaun'ae attack from the south."

"Why dae ye suppose what ye heard differs from what the history book says?"

"The druids were trying tae change history, and Donald was taking their counsel, aye? Perhaps this is the bit that needs tae change in order for Scotland tae become a world power through Donald."

"Aye, that makes sense. We need tae tell Leif."

"Is that enough? Here we be. I hae the opportunity tae end everything in the most obvious way."

Her body clenched up and she placed a hand on his arm. "What most obvious way? What dae ye speak o'?"

Talking over his shoulder with his back to her was putting a crimp in his neck. Surely she was reassured by now that he wasn't going to try anything. Luag turned onto his back, wriggling around the sword so it wasn't stabbing him in the bum. He had to lie atop it. He couldn't allow anyone to steal it from him, and it had to be within reach if someone tried something. "My uncle is sleeping, and everyone now kens he has welcomed me back. I could gae tae him, say I wished a word with him, and rush in afore they could wake him. I could end this once and for all."

She jumped on top of him and held him in an embrace that was even more startling than their kiss had been earlier. "Ye will na. 'Tis foolish! Ye would die yerself with the deed undone!" She clung to him, and then as an afterthought, she added, " And then where would I be? What would they do tae me?"

She was right.

He clung to her, holding her with as much abandon as she was holding him. And then he gently pushed her off him. "Katherine, I dinna trust myself with yer virtue a moment longer. Say ye wull stay ower on yer side o' the billet."

She was breathing heavy, and at first she started to reach out to him again. But sense took over and she nodded, rolling onto her stomach next to him on his back. This was a much more sensible arrangement for whispering to each other, and he was angry at himself for not thinking of it sooner.

16

Katherine's emotions were going up and down like a roller coaster. She couldn't keep up with them. Luag had just admitted he hadn't thought of what would happen to her if he went and got himself killed. She should be furious with him. Why wasn't she?

"Ye hae the right o' it, lass. We shall sleep, get up with the dawn, and steal away on the morrow amid the chaos o' beginning the march on Aberdeen."

For what seemed a long time, she tried to sleep. But it was useless.

"Are ye asleep?" she whispered.

"Nay. Are ye?"

"Nay," she whispered with a chuckle.

But Luag was quiet after that.

The only conclusion she could draw was he was

morose about once again leaving his people in order to fight against them. She could respect the sentiment, if not the wisdom of it. He was appreciated by Leif and Taran, and she felt like she needed to remind him of that.

"We have na whispered like this syne that night when little Amena was being sae funny. Remember?"

"Aye, such a joy tae watch her water all those imaginary flowers."

"She wanted ye in particular tae appreciate how pretty the flowers were, as I recall."

"Nay, she wished tae impress her brothers."

"Dinna be too sure aboot that. The lass is young, but in six more years ye may start tae feel differently aboot her."

Luag guffawed. "Och, she will never be anything but a sister tae me."

That memory was having the opposite effect from what she wanted, and so she tried a different one. "And ye are like a brother tae Leif and Taran. They include ye in all o' their plans. And as the odd woman oot tae yer odd man, I had the sore feet from many toon dances tae show for it."

He turned over on his side, putting his back to her once again. "I wish for ye tae pass a good night, Katherine."

Something was wrong. He didn't sound like someone eager to go back to his friends, but rather someone who thought he might miss them a long time. She brooded over that awhile before sleep finally took her.

In her dream, Katherine found Kelsey, Jessica, and Lauren inside the underground Alba palace at Dunskey castle. Through trial and error, Kelsey had discovered this was a safe place where she could protect dreams from intruders listening in. It was unclear why the druids had made Kelsey one of their own and given her such powers, but at times like this, Katherine was grateful for these powers. She ran first to hug Jessica, who she felt protective over, and then Lauren, who she had more in common with.

Having greeted her friends, she turned and gave Kelsey a grateful nod of thanks. "I'm surprised. It hasn't even been a week since the last time you brought us all into a dream. But it's a gift you did." She turned her attention on Jessica, Leif's wife. "Luag was welcomed here and he attended the war counsel. There, he found out Donald indeed plans on attacking Aberdeen. He's beginning the march tomorrow and should be there the next day, coming from the south."

"Are you sure?"

"There's nothing about Donald reaching Aberdeen in the history books."

"The Battle of Harlaw was the end of it."

"Aye, I'm sure," Katherine told them with as much emphasis as she could, giving them her level seven stare as well. She found that her level ten stare intimidated people too much. They shut down and didn't share with her anymore.

Jessica wrinkled her forehead. "Isn't it odd that Luag was accepted?"

"They nearly hanged him..."

When Katherine had related the whole story, she could tell she had sold them. They were ready to make plans. "Luag and I leave in the morning on horseback. We should be there by nightfall."

"We'll tell Alasdair," Jessica assured Katherine. "He's been able to win the Regent over. Kelsey, show her the hill we showed you."

Katherine had to resist the urge to lean back away from the dream chasm that opened up below her, showing the landscape as if she were flying over the road toward Aberdeen. Just before she reached the city on the east coast of Scotland, a hill rose up on the right. She soared down to where she could see a trail up the hill from the road, and then the chasm closed up and they were back in the underground palace beneath modern-day Dunskey Castle.

Lauren was pacing back and forth, obviously thinking through the ramifications. "We leave town in the morning and go make camp on that hill. Kelsey assures us we'll have a safe overview of the battle from up there and stay out of the way. Come find us."

Katherine nodded her agreement to this plan.

"I'll check in with you all after the battle just in case..." Kelsey didn't finish her thought, but Katherine understood. Just in case any of them lost their men and wanted to go home.

"I want to go home after the battle in any case," Katherine told their druid friend.

Kelsey nodded. "I'll be in touch."

Katherine drifted into a normal dream. About kissing Luag.

The morning was far more chaotic than when they arrived. Everyone was loading up provisions and larger weapons on the horses, putting out quick cooking fires, and pointing at where they should muster for the march.

She and Luag folded up their billet, took the plaid blanket down off the tree, and bundled it all up on the back of their own horse, then walked it out to the perimeter of all the camp activity.

"Dinna be proud," Luag told her. "Let me boost ye up."

How did he do that, know exactly when she was about to have a proud moment and resist a suggestion he made?

Giving him a look that said "verra well, I wull dae as ye say, but na because ye said it. I wull dae it because it makes sense, sae lose the idea ye can boss me around," she let him boost her up onto the horse.

He took an unusually long time doing so, lingering with her in his arms.

Once she was on horseback, there was barely any room behind her, what with the added bulk of the plaid blanket. Where was he going to sit?

He led the horse even more outside the perimeter of the camp, toward the road they'd come in on. "Dae ye recognize the way?"

"Aye," she told him. "'Tis just a straight shot along this road. It should na be difficult at all—"

Luag slapped Steam's rear, sending Katherine at a run toward the road without him.

17

L uag only allowed himself to watch Katherine on the horse until she was safely moving along the road. Luck had won and it was a market day, so wagonful after wagonful of produce was headed for the next town over. She would be well.

Thinking it was time to leave because he shouldn't let himself be caught sending her away, he turned around.

His heart nearly stopped.

Someone stood there.

Luag relaxed when he saw that it was Gehrig. Still, he stood and waited to see what the man would do.

Gehrig just nodded toward where they were supposed to go muster for the March. "Glad I am ye sent her away. That market toon is as good a place for her tae wait for ye as any."

Luag had put a few provisions from the saddlebags into his own knapsack. He adjusted it, and his sword, on his back and joined Gehrig to muster for the march. When they arrived, everyone else stood in formation, waiting.

Donald beckoned.

Before going to join his uncle, Luag gave Gehrig the slightest shrug of apology. "See ye at the midday meal."

Donald sat his horse proudly and patiently until Luag was beside him. "Now that my nephew has decided tae get up for the morning, we can leave!"

Everyone forced themselves to laugh.

Donald turned to Luag. "I see ye hae misplaced yer horse and yer wife."

Luag didn't have an answer. Knowing his uncle, he just remained silent.

Donald gave a small shake of his head. "Na matter." He turned to a young aide Luag thought might be the son of Gwendolyn. "Get Luag a horse tae ride, and be quick aboot it."

The young warrior ran off.

Donald appraised Luag. "At least ye hae the presence o' mind tae keep some vittles aboot ye. Otherwise I would be calling ye a fool, giving yer wife yer horse. Na matter. I shall be honored if ye take yer meals with me."

That oily feeling took to Luag's skin again. The urge to try and rub off his uncle's cloying indulgence was almost unbearable. Thankfully, a horse soon appeared, and Luag mounted, happy to ride, at least, rather than stand there under scrutiny.

The army began its two-day march on Aberdeen.

Riding next to his uncle was hardly a treat. The man's comments made Luag uncomfortable. The other clan chieftains rode near, and Donald kept up a constant conversation with them.

"Och, how wull they march."

"Aye, this time we wull hae the prize."

"Nay thanks tae Roland."

"We hae na need o' the puny druid. He has served his purpose in telling us what must be done, but we who are indeed men need tae dae it." This was met with uproarious laughter every time it was said.

"They will na ken what has struck them."

"Aye, they are ripe for the taking."

Luag grinned and bore with it. Riding with these people would have been an entirely distasteful experience except for one fact. Roland was right. From the soaring heights of the gray stone-top mountains to the vast expanses of meadow between them and the waterfalls that graced the rivers and streams, everything about this land inspired awe. Having seen modern man-made monstrosities and wonders, Luag appreciated Scottish scenery as he never had before. It was his one pleasure on this forsaken journey. And it must be preserved.

At the midday meal —which Luag was now cursed to spend far away from Gehrig—Uncle's boasting became even more unbearable.

"We shall take them unawares, and Aberdeen will be mine. Just the next step upon my ladder tae glory as king o' Scotland. I could na dae it with nary all o' ye." He smiled at his sycophants. "And therefore, ye will all hae prominent places in my kingdom."

"Long live the king!"

"May he reign in majesty glorious."

Never in all this revelry did anyone look at Luag. Oh, Donald glanced his way now and then, appearing to include Luag in his assurance that everyone who had helped him would be part of his kingdom. But his uncle never did meet Luag's eyes, even though Luag was seated prominently on his right with Donald's current young wife on his left.

All this only solidified Luag's conviction that had been right to leave his clan and join Leif's. Uncle was an insufferable arrogant oaf, and Luag looked forward to his defeat at Aberdeen with great relish, even though Luag would be entirely too close to the action.

Donald must have guessed Luag's plan to turn his cousins against the cause, because his uncle kept Luag with him always.

"Yer rightful place is beside me, Nephew. Ride with me."

Once darkness was near, they made camp. Donald called an even more elaborate evening meal with not only all the other clan chiefs, but also their wives and aides. Hunting parties had returned with deer, and It was a celebratory feast before the battle had even taken place.

Luag wanted no part of it, but he knew what he'd signed up for. If he was going to pretend to be back in the clan, that meant nodding and smiling at all of his uncle's braggery.

"Once I am king," said Donald, "I will award ye all lairdships. Be thinking aboot which castle ye wish tae be laird o', because ye shall hae it, each and every one o' ye." Once again, Donald's glance glazed over Luag but didn't quite settle on him.

Luag felt uneasy. This was over-the-top even for his uncle, to be so secure in the confidence of his victory before battle.

Later that evening, Donald's young and beautiful

current wife approached where the clan chieftains sat around the fire together, toasting each other's battle prowess.

"Husband, 'tis time tae retire."

Donald raised his eyebrows and gave a heavy wink as he looped his wife's arm through his and headed off to their tent.

Finally, Luag had his chance. He stood up and toasted the chiefs with his tankard and turned as if he were going off to bed as well, walking toward his billet until he heard them laughing and joking among themselves behind him once more. Only then did he head off to find his cousins.

Luag approached the fire where his cousin Bran sat joking with others their age. Luag had trouble meeting Bran's eyes, so Luag moved closer into the fire circle and sat down across from him. While Luag waited for his cousin to realize he was there, he listened to what they had to say.

"Gaun'ae be an easy battle."

"Aye. The lowlanders are na match for us."

"Anyone who puts his trust in them is foolish."

Luag's temper rose at the slights to Leif's people, and his cousin still hadn't looked him in the eye and acknowledged his presence.

Luag stood up.

As the only one standing in the fire circle, he was

clearly visible. He held his position there for a few moments, but it became clear what was happening.

Bran was shunning him.

It was pointless to try and say anything, so Luag left.

He had a similar experience around his cousin Searc's fire.

Luag slumped off to where he had lain his billet next to Gehrig's.

But he couldn't find his billet. He looked everywhere.

Finally, Igor showed up and told him, "Ye hae been moved ower near Laird Donald's tent."

LUAG WAS BACK INSIDE THE MARVELOUS CASTLE-like hotel with Katherine, calling for room service.

Katherine was watching him do so, looking proud. Her beautiful hair hung down loose about her face, and she wore one of those skimpy outfits so common in her time.

He smiled at her and raised his eyebrows as if to say 'See? I can learn.'

She gave him a very satisfying nod of agreement that made him warm inside like none of his uncle's empty praise ever could.

He put the phone down. "I took your advice and ordered from the menu this time."

She took a step closer to him. Just one step, but it made his heart race and his skin feel warm. "Oh yeah? What should I look forward to having?"

Was that yearning he saw in her eyes, or was he just feeding into her expression the way he felt? "Verra soon, we will be dining on spaghetti with meatballs, accompanied by garlic bread and corn on the cob."

In that adorable way she had, she suppressed a grin at his expense. "And do you have any idea what all that is?"

Testing a theory, he went over and sat down on a chair at the small table, a few feet nearer to her than he had been before.

It worked. She came and sat down beside him, so close that if he reached out, he could touch her. But he didn't. What was the hurry? It was so nice just to have her here by his side. They were young. They had all the time in the world. This was all he needed right now. They sat there at the table smiling at each other.

While it wasn't awkward at all, he felt a cloying tension grow in the air, his desire to reach over and touch her became so urgent. Again, what was the hurry?

The hotel suite's television droned on, some story about a man in the jungle, fighting monsters called alligators. Luag and Katherine listened to the story, but they were watching each other's faces, smiling together at the comical parts and grimacing in horror together with the man was in peril.

It was more fun than Luag had ever had.

There was a knock at the door. "Room service."

The food was delicious, and they concentrated on eating, only exchanging pleasantries.

"I find I quite like spaghetti and meatballs."

"How about the garlic bread and corn?"

He wanted to tell her that her company would make anything taste good, but he found his normal wit didn't seem appropriate in this moment. He just wanted to enjoy her closeness while he could.

His instincts told him there was a reason he ought to savor each and every moment with Katherine, but he couldn't think what that might be. It nagged at him, this feeling that he had better enjoy these moments with her because... No, try as he might, he just couldn't think why their time together would be limited.

He did enjoy these moments with her, stealing glances while she ate.

She excused herself and went to the restroom.

He thought he'd go check on Roland, but then he

knew somehow that Roland wasn't in the next room, and it didn't distress him. Why not?

Katherine was back, and all thoughts of anything else left him. She was breathtakingly beautiful, and he felt drawn to her the way he had never felt drawn to anyone before.

He went to her, holding out his arms for her to walk into his embrace.

She did.

They settled onto the couch in each other's arms and watched the TV together in cozy comfort.

Holding her close made him feel like finally, he had a home.

***

"KATHERINE, YE FELL ASLEEP ON MY ARM AND 'tis killing me. Wake up."

Luag opened his eyes to the starry night sky with just a hint of dawn. He felt around him for Katherine, certain he would find her there by his side where she belonged.

But then full wakefulness took hold of him and he remembered. He'd sent her away. And for good reason. He needed to see a friendly face, and now was his chance, before the camp awoke. He quickly packed up his billet onto his horse and went to find Gehrig.

Everyone's resolve to pointedly ignore Luag served him well here. Uncle's guards let him walk right past them away from his billet near Donald's tent to where the common soldiers lay asleep. The guards on watch there ignored him too.

He entered their camp, knelt down by Gehrig, and shook his shoulder a bit.

"Gehrig, wake up. This may be oor only chance tae speak."

Gehrig's eyes opened and he stretched. He met Luag's eyes, but he didn't smile or say a word in greeting. As he packed up his things onto his back, he merely nodded toward where the aroma of some aught to break the men's fast wafted over.

Luag fell in beside him, and as they walked the short distance, they had a short whispered conversation.

"Wish I were marching with ye instead o' riding with my uncle."

"Nay, ye dinna."

"Why na?"

"Na matter what anyone says, everyone still thinks ye a traitor."

❧ 18 ❧

Katherine had tears streaming down her face when she finally rode into Jessica and Lauren's camp on the hill west of Aberdeen. Indeed, she'd had tears streaming down her face throughout the whole ride here.

Lauren grabbed the reins while Katherine climbed down. "What's wrong? Did Luag get in a fight? Where is he?"

Katherine fell into Lauren's arms as soon as she dismounted. "No, no, nothing like that. He's still with Donald. Still trying to enact his original plan of getting his MacDonald cousins to defect with those loyal to them. He said he was coming with me and then once I was on the horse, he slapped it."

Jessica came and took Katherine's other hand

and together with Lauren led her to a seating area they had created.

Through her tears, Katherine looked out over Aberdeen. They could see the whole city, all of its gates and activity, plus dozens of ships in the harbor.

Still sniffling, Katherine nodded at them in thanks and took a seat. "I didn't want to care about him this much. He kissed me. We shared a tent, and we cuddled. It was wonderful. But now the idea of him among those who hate him so while he's trying to help us hurts me to my core. When I was just going home, I could imagine him here with you, having the life he deserves."

Jessica massaged Katherine's shoulder with one hand and took hold of her hand with the other. "I'm glad you're back, Katherine. We were so worried about you. He's doing what he can to keep everyone here safe. That's why you care about him."

Their attempts to console her only made Katherine cry harder.

They put their arms around her and let her cry awhile.

While she cried, she watched the action below. Aberdeen's people were manning the walls and gates with bows and arrows. Knights in chainmail patrolled outside the wall. Inverurie's militia had shown up. Leif and Taran were with them at the south gate where the action would be, swords and pikes ready, a large pile of stones at hand.

All those people down there were risking their lives to defend their home from something they had no control over, and she was worried about one man who had gone to be with the enemy of his own choice. She needed to pull herself together.

"The defense looks good," she told Jessica with a smile. "Leif and Taran know what they're about, and everyone's busy doing as they say. That's a good sign." She wiped the last tears from her face using the back of her hand and gave Jessica her most reassuring look.

Jessica squeezed her hand. "Aye, those people down there are doing their best to fortify the city, and they're doing a good job."

Katherine put a hand on Jessica's arm. "You don't sound so sure. Why not?"

Lauren put her arm around Jessica and patted her back. "Alasdair and his knights haven't shown up yet, and they constitute most of the forces at our disposal."

Worry seeped its way back into Katherine's mind. "Where are they?"

One tear escaped down Jessica's cheek. She let it stay, visibly trying to look ladylike. "No one knows." A single sob escaped Jessica's mouth. "Alasdair sounded so supportive. I thought he believed us."

Lauren held her sister-in-law close.

Jessica closed her eyes, visibly fighting the tears and sobs but losing so far.

A tiny bit of anger came to Katherine's rescue, allowing her to at last banish the tears. "I thought Alasdair believed us too." She turned toward her friends. "Do you think we should go down inside the city and help defend the walls? We can throw stones just as well as anybody else—"

"No!" her friends said at the same time.

Katherine raised an eyebrow at Lauren, the stronger of the two. "Why not?"

"Believe me, we've been over and over that with our husbands. They're both adamant that we stay out of harm's way, else they will worry about us too much and their heads won't be clear."

Katherine held up her hand, surrendering the point. "You're right. I can see that. Besides, without Galdus you're as useless in a fight as Jessica and me, right?"

Lauren pressed her lips together and inclined her head. "Right. At times like this, I regret giving him up."

Jessica was still sobbing, but she snapped to attention and grabbed Lauren's hand. "Nonsense.

Galdus was taking control of you. Don't even talk like that. You did what you had to do, and we're all glad."

Leif and Taran were drilling the militia. Over and over, they would throw the stones over the wall in strategic locations, then run out to gather them up again, piling them behind the wall. The city folk drilled as well, even the women with bows, but they didn't shoot their arrows, saving them all for actual combat.

Katherine was ashamed, watching the women prepare to help defend their home. She'd been here a year. She could have learned how to shoot arrows. What had she been up to? Not much, that was what. So what if she knew who Leif's contacts were in all the cities of Scotland, their names, their families' names, their likes and dislikes? Who did she think she was, a lady herself? No, she was just a commoner, and all the commoners down there in Aberdeen knew how to defend their home.

Which begged the question in the back of her mind.

"Jessica, where are the other ladies?"

Jessica smiled, but she looked worried. "They all stayed in the Regent's residence. They said it was the safest place for them."

An unwelcome thought came to Katherine, and

she felt like she had to share it, that it would be irresponsible not to. "What are we supposed to do if..."

Jessica took a deep breath and looked off into the distance, away from Aberdeen. "If the city gets overrun, we are to go higher up into the mountains, wait for Kelsey to contact us in her dreams, and ask her to get us home to the 21st Century."

Katherine squeezed Jessica's hand. "I'm sorry I had to ask that, but—"

Jessica squeezed her hand back. "Don't worry about it. It makes sense to have a plan. They don't want to worry about us. They want us to be safe no matter what, and so they thought of that too. Shows how much they love us." Jessica lost her battle with the sobs then.

As Katherine moved in to comfort her friend, a lot of movement off to the left caught her eye.

"What's that?"

"What?" Lauren asked, turning her head also to the left to look —and opening her eyes wide once she had.

All three women screamed.

A great horde of warriors came running toward the sparsely guarded northern wall and gates of Aberdeen.

❈ 19 ❈

uag watched for his chance. While they were all riding together was not the time. Too much chance that someone would stop him. He had to wait until they were in an open field, and the area north of Aberdeen —toward which he had realized some time ago they were headed— was open, indeed. That was where he would do it.

It was difficult, biding his time until then, pretending so much. Pretending to share in the enthusiasm of his uncle's boasts. "We wull hae our victory afore the fall o' night, ye ken!" Pretending not to realize his uncle had lied about coming from the south when he intended all along to attack Aberdeen from the north.

Luag found what solace he could in the knowledge that at least he had been instrumental in getting Roland to dissuade the druids from taking part in his uncle's war campaign.

At long last, Donald's army arrived at the open space north of Aberdeen and broke into a run, throwing everything into chaos. Now was his chance. Now was the time when the fewest would see.

Drawing his weapon like everyone else had, Luag charged his horse directly at his uncle's. Not at his back. No, that was the coward's way out. Luag charged Donald straight on, face to face, sword raised in an obvious threat, his intent clear.

Against all reason and instinct for caution, Luag also called out a challenge. "Ye played me false, Uncle!"

Donald's many lackeys turned to cut Luag off.

No matter. Luag was not going to restrain himself one more moment. Far better to die fighting his enemy than any other way.

But Donald raised a hand to halt his men, calling out his own challenge. "Ye hae also played me false, Nephew."

The truth of this hit Luag in the gut, but he had no more remorse than that. "'Tis true, sae let us fight this oot."

The two of them rode by each other, each

striking at the other in an attempt to knock the other from his horse, and each failing.

Lackeys had begun to crowd around, making a hubbub of speculation about how soon their laird would strike his nephew down, and how bloody it would be.

But Donald reared his horse up at them and put an end to that. "Ye hae a battle tae fight. Gae tae it."

They hastened away, the fear in their eyes reinforcing Luag's resolve.

His uncle's difficulty with his men wasn't going to stop Luag from making another charge. He turned his horse in the damp rain-soaked soil and then started it, hoofs pounding under him and his weapon held firmly in his outstretched hand.

Donald met the challenge fiercely, holding his own weapon out while leering at Luag and calling out to his men, "Leave us!"

The two clashed again.

Luag drove his sword toward Donald's as hard as he could. A strong jab should do it. Aye! He struck his uncle's weapon in such a way that it went flying out of the man's hand.

But that victory was short-lived. Donald drew another weapon and turned to make another charge.

It took ten charges before they were both on their

feet, their horses settling down to graze the lush tall grass together a few yards off.

Fighting on foot was much more satisfying. He could see his uncle's hateful eyes up close and personal, just the way he needed to in order to end the man who wanted to be king despite the best interests of Scotland.

"Ye think tae best me again, Uncle, but ye are aulder now and getting frail, betimes I am in my prime." Luag lunged at the enemy's gut with all his strength.

But Donald easily evaded Luag's thrust and followed through with one of his own. "And ye hae been spending yer time among soft lowlanders, while I hae always carried on in fighting the best warriors."

Luag hacked and thrust with all he had, but his uncle refused to die. The two were evenly matched.

As they fought, Luag was aware that Donald's horde of islander Viking warriors was swarming the walls of Aberdeen. He didn't hold out much hope that the city would be able to resist.

But if he could just end his uncle, the bloodbath would slow down immensely. He wasn't foolish enough to think the Scots could ever stop fighting each other, but an end to his uncle's campaign to be king would do. Aye, it would do nicely.

Luag was mid-charge at Donald when he heard the bagpipes.

Donald heard them too, because his face was stricken with urgent worry.

Accompanied by the rallying call of the pipes, Alasdair and his knights rode down from the western hills toward the northern wall of Aberdeen, moving through Donald's horde of warriors as they did, scything them left and right, forming a wedge between the enemy and the walls, churning and spraying blood.

The tide had turned.

Donald's nearest lackeys were urging on the ranks from the rear, shouting for them to go faster even as the ranks in the front died left and right at the onslaught of mounted man in chain armor.

Calling out to his lackeys, "Sound the retreat," Donald turned and fled like the coward he was.

His men cursed him, but they followed.

Luag was tempted to stand his ground and watch everyone run past him, giving them gloating looks. But he was no fool. Unlike the knights Alasdair led, he wore only wool: a Gaelic plaid and a Viking animal pattern.

He got on his horse and rode for the western hills, expecting to be followed and cut down.

Luag spotted the camp at the top of the hill and turned cautious, keeping the horse to the cover of the trees rather than ride out in the open where he could go faster. Was it friend or foe? Did he have any friends left?

The backside of the hill was devoid of trees, and whoever was up in this camp would've had a nice view of the battlefield. Had they only watched Aberdeen nearly fall but then triumph, or had they seen him challenging a despot? Would it matter?

He needed to know who was up there. He couldn't let them follow him and cut him down unawares. Far better to face them head on, so he kept up his relentless ride toward the camp.

Wait, was that Leif's plaid he saw over the tree? Luag's stomach churned with excitement, both at the idea that his friend was up here and also the idea of seeing him again, having someone to come home to. He hurried his horse up the rest of the hill, and sure enough that was Leif's plaid.

"Leif, are ye there?"

Luag's heart beat even faster than it had while he fought, he was so anxious to see a friendly face.

The plaid leapt about with the activity of people

behind it. Was all well? Had attackers made their way up here and killed his friends?

Luag jumped down from his horse, gave it the command to graze, and ran through the trees toward the tent with his sword out, desperate to save the lives of whoever he could from the attackers.

The voice he heard melted his heart.

"Luag, could it be ye?"

And there she was, the only lass he had ever loved as a man loves a lass. The sunlight found its way to her fair hair and glinted off like gold. Her eyes sparkled like the waters of the sea under that same sunlight.

And then she was crushing him in her arms and he was kissing her.

She returned his kiss for a few ecstatic moments, then broke away, holding him at arms' length and plainly searching him for blood. "I could hae killed ye when ye sent me off by myself. What were ye thinking?"

He loved it when she got just a bit cross with him. It made her eyes sparkle all the more, and her body move with exciting precision.

"It doesna matter. Aberdeen is safe..."

As he told her this, he became aware of Jessica and Lauren fidgeting in the tent away from his and Katherine's reunion. "Now the matter at hand is to find out if Leif and Taran are safe. Come, let us go doon—"

Jessica and Lauren both rushed out, looking worried but determined.

Lauren made the cutting gesture. "They will come here at the first opportunity. We hae strict orders tae stay and wait, though I suppose that does na include ye and Katherine."

Luag looked over at the lasses his dear friends Leif and Taran had married. "They are like brothers tae me, and sae ye are like sisters. We are family, and I wull bide here with ye."

Katherine had been clinging to his side, but now she moved away and went to stand with the other lasses. Common sense told him it was because he and she no longer had privacy, but from his time in the future at her home, he knew that wasn't it.

She put her arms around both the other lasses. "Luag, give us a charade tae entertain us while we wait, aye?"

* * *

THE LASSES HAD BEEN SLOW TO GET INTO THE game at first, but this was Lauren's favorite game, so she at least had jumped into it with vigor once he got started, winning ten of the twenty turns they had taken. She was currently up. The other lasses were guessing, and Luag was doing his best to let them win. They were the ones who needed the distraction.

He saw signs of a small party coming up the hill toward the camp before the lasses did. The trees moved just a bit, and birds took flight and called to each other. It was probably Leif and Taran, but until Luag was sure, he kept his weapon hand free and himself away from having a turn at Charades.

A good sign was that whoever was coming wasn't being aggressive about it. He would have known because of the birds flying away. However, Luag subtly moved himself between the lasses and those who approached.

It would do no good to warn the lasses an enemy might be approaching. None of them were warriors, and there was nowhere for them to take refuge. Their panic might ignite aggression in whoever approached.

He mustn't have hidden his intentions well enough though, because Lauren called him out on it. "Someone's coming, are na they, Luag."

He held up his hands in the sign for remaining still and then signed to them, "'Tis probably yer husbands, but till we ken for certies, please remain quiet and stay behind me sae that I can defend ye."

To his surprise, the lasses nodded in agreement

and did as he said, waiting in silence for several more moments.

The sound of Leif's smallpipes wafted up from below with the signal that meant "All is well."

Luag grabbed Katherine's hand and went running to greet the rest of his family.

They had just finished picking up Jessica and Lauren's camp when it hit Katherine. It was time for her to go. What she had come to accomplish, she had done.

She looked for an opportunity to get Lauren alone, and while Jessica checked how well the men had packed the camp stuff onto Luag's horse, she got it.

Taran and Leif were filling Luag in on their side of the battle.

"People on the wall, who saw Donald's army coming, alerted us in time."

"Aye, we all grabbed two stones each and ran ower there."

"Every man in the militia can lay claim tae having hit maire than one MacDonald sympathizer."

Katherine met Lauren's eye and inclined her head down the hill to where their seats had been arranged for watching the battle.

Looking very curious, Lauren raised an eyebrow and followed her there. "What is it?"

Katherine gazed down and watched Aberdeen's people clean up the debris of the battle. "Is there a way ye can help me get away withoot being noticed?"

Lauren took hold of Katherine's shoulder and pulled her around to see Lauren's frown. "Why?"

Katherine caught herself looking up the hill to watch Luag.

His face was glorious as he loudly related his end of the battle to his adopted brothers. "'Twas Uncle who backed down from the fight. I was victorious. My only regret is na ending him when I had the chance, but ye saw him retreat."

Leif clapped him on the back. "The men on the wall saw it."

Taran reached out and embraced forearms with Luag. "Ye did well, and we all thank ye for it, howso-ever, ye should hae come home with Katherine."

Luag looked up and met Katherine's eyes then.

She almost lost her resolve to go home.

His look was so loving, so inviting. It told her that any minute now, he would ask her to be his wife — and that he was certain she would say yes.

But he didn't do it at this moment, and so she escaped. No, he went back to his conversation about the battle.

That gave Katherine her chance to escape him. Keeping her eyes on him the entire time —memorizing his face, the way he moved, the cadence of his voice— she made her appeal. "Lauren, I canna bide in this time. 'Tis verra happy I am for ye, being able tae adapt, tae love living here in 1411, but it is na for me. I need tae go. Verra soon, he wull ask me tae stay. I canna hurt him by saying nay, and I will na ask him tae come home with me. He was miserable in our time."

Lauren hugged Katherine, and while they were still holding each other tight, whispered, "Aye, I wull distract them while ye go on doon tae the inn and get yerself a room. We gae home tae Inverurie this verra day. Kelsey said she would contact us all this night."

Katherine squeezed Lauren's hands. "Just in case, I think I'd better get a room in a different inn."

Lauren pulled away with a sad smile. "Aye, ye hae the right o' it."

⁊

SURE ENOUGH, THAT NIGHT KATHERINE FOUND herself in the Dunskey Castle dream. A new woman was there, someone Katherine didn't know, but who obviously knew Kelsey and Lauren well.

Kelsey met Katherine's eyes. "Katherine, this is Sarah. Sarah, this is Katherine."

Sarah threw up her hands in exasperation but spared a brief "Hi Katherine" before turning back to Kelsey. "I'm telling you, Michael doesn't need to be at Celtic University. Why can't you get him to check in somewhere else? I love my job here and it's going so well, but having him here is too much of a distraction."

Kelsey held up her hand for quiet. "I thought I could keep you here for this, but obviously I can't. I'll talk to you later."

Sarah's exasperation was almost comical as she faded out of the dream.

"Sorry about that," Kelsey said, giving Katherine an apologetic smile that attempted to hide her amusement at Sarah's predicament. "I understand you want to go home to the future."

"Thank you," Katherine told her. "Yes, I do. Right away. As soon as possible. Did Lauren tell you why, or does it matter?"

Kelsey wrinkled her nose in a fair imitation of Katherine's most effective facial expression for sales, making Katherine chuckle a bit. "Yes, Lauren explained everything. It's raised my opinion of you considerably, you selflessly taking yourself out of Luag's life before you can hurt his feelings too much by saying no. I will arrange for Roland Cheyne to meet you first thing in the morning."

Katherine gasped. "You know him?"

Kelsey lowered her chin. "We do now. The future made quite an impression on him, and he has reached out to us. But he will not come into Aberdeen to meet you, ye ken. Meet him back up on that hill west of town."

SCOTLAND WAS UNFAIRLY BEAUTIFUL IN THE morning. The sun was out for once, glistening on the dewy grass and thistles, highlighting the purple Heather out in the fields and the grey stones at the top of the mountains. Just the right amount of thundercloud lurked behind those mountains, rumbling majestically.

Katherine drank in the scenery while she could.

A small part of her, the selfish part, kept expecting Luag to appear. Her selfish mind even worked out a scene the two of them would play out when he did.

"Katherine, ye mean the waurld tae me. Wherever ye go, I wish tae follow. I dinna care if that means leaving my waurld and all that is familiar tae me. Yer love will be enough. Ye are enough for me. Let's make a family together."

She embraced him then, and they shared one of those kisses that made her toes curl.

But Katherine knew that was the selfish part of her thinking, so she only looked for him ten of the thirty times she wanted to, hoping to catch sight of him following her, urgent to catch up with her before she left. He had to know she was leaving. Lauren would've told him by now. But realistically, Luag was halfway back to Inverurie now, already thinking about how to train the militia for the next battle that would surely come.

If she had learned anything from reading that book about Inverurie's history, it was that battle after battle with each other was the story of Scotland's life. If only she could convince them that the English were their true enemies.

As she walked out on what had been a battlefield the day before, the sun continued to rise, glinting off the occasional weapon dropped in the heat of battle —or more likely in the heat of retreat. Aye battle was Scotland's history, and the Scottish men got their grit from it. They wouldn't be as attractive without it, was the sad truth. Without battle, Scottish men from history would look just like American men from her time.

These conflicting thoughts warbled through her mind as she surveyed the green meadow and surrounding grey mountains with their angry storm cloud background for the last time. Best to think of this past year as a vacation. A few pictures couldn't hurt, out here were no one else could see her, right? She got out her phone and took a panoramic video that she could pull stills from later, featuring Aberdeen in its medieval state with nary a neon sign in site.

Because after all, these mountains and meadows were preserved in her time, weren't they. If she wanted to, she could visit them.

She had helped to ensure that.

It was almost as good as being with Luag.

Yes. Yes, it was. She was firm with herself on this, because the alternative was tears, and that was the last thing she needed right before returning home and having to face her responsible job. The CEOs of survival supply companies wouldn't buy from a blubbering fool.

She heard a twig snap behind her, and her heart raced.

Now that he was right behind her, all her resolve to let him go disappeared.

Maybe Kelsey would help them visit each other. It would be the longest distance relationship she'd ever heard of, but... She couldn't be gone from her job for more than a weekend, but...

Her conscience told her this was ridiculous. What if you have children? Are you going to bring them back here to visit their father, modern children who would be in constant peril from not knowing how to live in these times?

But she ignored her conscience. Filled with hope, passion and an amount of desire she'd never known before, Katherine turned to welcome Luag into her arms.

But it was only Roland.

Deflated, she mustered the best smile she could to greet him.

Maybe reading minds was his druid gift, because he smiled at her in sympathy. "I'm here tae help ye go home tae yer time. I wull na be coming with ye, ye ken. I will open up a portal and ye wull just step through. I wull put ye inside yer apartment."

Katherine said anything she could think of to disguise her disappointment that it wasn't Luag. "Ye can open a portal right intae my apartment?"

He smiled like someone who had the keys to the Mercedes factory. "Here in a sacred grove that still exists thanks tae yer help, aye, I can."

"Ye have na been in my apartment. What's tae stop other druids from opening up portals there?"

"Aye, but ye hae been in yer apartment, and I hae touched ye. Only one other druid has done sae, aye? Kelsey is the only other druid who could dae sae, if she had the ability tae open portals, which she does na. Yet."

Katherine relaxed. It was comforting, the idea that Kelsey would still be in her life. That meant Jessica and Lauren could help her keep tabs on Luag in her dreams. It would be enough.

She gave Roland a smile of thanks. "I'm ready. Take me tae this sacred grove o' yers and get me home."

&

HER APARTMENT SMELLED SO STALE, SHE RAN and opened all the windows, muttering to herself about fresh air and pollution. She didn't own any plants, and she would have to change that during the trip she would make to the farmers market this evening.

It was the same time here as it had been in 1411: six in the morning on what promised to be a scorching July day, even in this beach town.

She texted her boss. "I'm back. I'll be in today, but

later. Need to do some personal errands. See you this afternoon." She called her salon and arranged for the full treatment: hair, skin, and nails. Next, she went to her closet and found something that had been dry cleaned and was classic, so being more than a year old wouldn't be an issue.

With her Brooks Brothers suit safely in her garment bag and wearing shorts and a cute tank top, she went downstairs to the café for her ritual morning nonfat cinnamon latte.

Oh good, Lupe was here.

And slightly cross. "You said I'd see you on Tuesday, Chica. Where did you have breakfast yesterday and the day before?" But Lupe's smile betrayed her amusement.

Katherine went behind the counter to embrace her favorite barista. "I missed you too. I had some things I had to take care of, so I went away for a few days. But now I truly am home. The next time I go away, I'll tell you ahead of time, okay?"

"Okay," Lupe told her with a wink while she got started on Katherine's latte, "and by the way, this is my brother, Ignacio. I think you two have met already. Sorry about that."

Ignacio was the man who had kicked Luag out. He smiled at Katherine. "No hard feelings, I hope." He held out his hand.

She shook it. "No hard feelings. I'm glad to meet you, Ignacio."

She took her latte over to her favorite table and plugged in her phone to charge while she slurped. It tasted like home.

❧ 21 ❧

F ortified with protein and caffeine, Katherine ordered an Uber to her salon. It would be here in half an hour. Might as well better familiarize herself with PenUlt's new products. She could personally attest to how good the backpack was, but she hadn't had time to test the cell phone earrings. She put them in and called Kelsey, using the number she'd found on Celtic University's website.

"Kelsey MacGregor."

"Hi Kelsey, it's Katherine."

"I'm so glad you made it home, but can we chat some other time? This thing with Sarah and Michael is taking up all my time today. Sorry."

"No problem," Katherine told Kelsey, tapping her

earring to disconnect the call. Wow, these earrings worked great!

Inexplicably, Lupe gasped at the sound of the door opening. The barista was so level headed, this caused Katherine to look away from the latte she was savoring, having only a few swallows left.

What?

Luag stood there in the door to the café.

Katherine hadn't done any makeup, being on her way to the salon, and so she was able to rub her eyes, thank goodness. She had to pull herself together.

But when she opened her eyes again, Luag still stood there, waiting for her to acknowledge him.

Lupe beat her to it. "Come on in, Luag."

Luag smiled at Lupe and inclined his head to Ignacio as he entered the café, but he didn't come over to Katherine. He was still giving her the chance to welcome him, or not.

Katherine stood up. "Luag, why have you come for a visit? Is everything okay? Please tell me no one died." She held her breath while Luag approached her.

His face didn't look worried, so it was good news. Was Jessica pregnant? Was Lauren pregnant? Yes, that was probably it. He looked excited, eager.

She felt herself fidgeting with her latte cup, pulling the lid off and pushing it on, slushing the small amount of liquid around. Unable to contain herself —unusual for her— she blurted out, "What's the news? Just tell me already. The suspense is killing me."

Lupe and Ignacio both laughed. And so did all the customers.

"What's going on?" Katherine asked Lupe.

Unexpectedly, Luag answered. "I've been here two hours, just to make sure I caught ye before work this morning. I already had a nice conversation with Lupe and Ignacio and everybody here. They're laughing because they ken I've come all the way from Scotland just to see ye."

Hope sprouted in Katherine's heart. She looked up into Luag's eyes and saw only him, shutting out everyone else —for now. She was certainly going to have a word with Lupe later.

But old reactions died hard, and having to look up at him vexed her even now.

When she stood, she was still looking at his chest, but that was better than when she'd been sitting down. "Oh?" she said. "Pray tell, Luag, why have you come all this way from Scotland just to see little old me?" She put on a Scottish accent. "Are na they keeping ye busy enough in Scotland?"

He came right up and put his arms around her, resting his hands on her waist and moving his face close enough to kiss her. "I came to ask you a verra important question, lass."

She wanted to be flippant, to make everyone laugh with her the way they'd laughed with him.

But his eyes stopped her from joking this time. They had been aloof most of the time she'd known him, reserved. But now, so close to hers, she could see they were beseeching. And fearful.

That sprout of hope in her heart blossomed, and her body urged her to close the distance and kiss him already.

But she had to make sure he'd thought this through. "But you were miserable here in my time, Luag."

He raised his eyebrows and cast his eyes about the room at the other people.

Still lost in his deep blue eyes, she quickly amended, "Here in America, I mean. You were here all of two days and you hated it. I would've invited you to come back with me from Scotland except for that. And what about Leif and Taran? Don't they need you? You were training—"

Still with his face kissing close, he interrupted. "They're as good as I am now. And I ken ye would na be happy living in Scotland."

It took all her will to stop herself from kissing

him. She sensed he had something to say, and she didn't want to stop him from saying it.

He kissed the air in front of her and then smiled at her mischievously before he spoke some more. "I will na be happy without ye, Katherine."

"Well," she told him with a grin, "I have it on good authority that 'The best way tae dae some aught difficult is as fast as ye can.'"

Her quip visibly softened his fear, bringing back more of the warrior she so desired. His shoulders went back and his chest filled out with pride in his ability to conquer.

His voice was soft, only for her ears, making her feel higher than a kite. "Verra well. I came to ask you to be my wife, Katherine, to take intae yer home for the rest of our lives, if you'll have me."

She couldn't help it. "Had na you better ask me, then?"

Close-up like this, only she could see the promise of an equally hard time for her in his eyes when he said, "Will ye be my wife, Katherine?"

"Aye, I will—"

She was going to say more, but he crushed her in a hug and kiss.

Everyone around clapped and cheered, then rushed to congratulate them. Lupe took pictures, and Ignacio served cake. Thankfully, someone had explained to Luag he could keep his arm around her the whole time.

With him so attached to her, Katherine asked Lupe, "Do you know a father who could marry us today?"

Lupe gave Katherine a knowing look. "I do, but there's a mandatory waiting time in California, and a blood test requirement. So you can wait, or you can go to Vegas."

Katherine must've looked crestfallen, because Ignacio spoke. "I have a spare room Luag can have until you get married. It's close by, so you can see each other most of the time."

"That's perfect," Lupe chimed in. "We already know you work together." She turned to Luag. "Say yes."

Laughing, Luag said, "Yes."

"Oh no."

Everyone looked at Katherine.

"Our Uber's here. We have to go."

Luag got the full treatment right next to her, and everyone in the salon commented about her sexy spa date. She bought him some slacks and a designer shirt, and finally the two of them were polished and coiffed and ready to go talk to her boss.

Michelle waved them right into Kate's office.

Kate was sitting at her huge desk, and her face lit up when she saw Katherine, but even more so when she saw Luag. "Now I see what's kept you so busy this past year." She ended this with a wink meant to unsettle Katherine.

It didn't work.

"We have other news, Kate. I'll let Luag tell you. Luag this is Kate, my boss. Kate, this is Luag."

Kate's amused eyes were on Katherine until she heard Luag's Scottish accent.

"'Tis glad I am to meet ye, Kate."

Kate was on their side of her desk in a split-second, holding out her hand for a handshake. "Pleased to meet you, indeed." She looked Luag up and down.

Luag went for the forearm grasp.

Katherine winced.

But Kate laughed and clasped Luag's forearm as well. "I don't remember this practice from our visit to Scotland, but it's charming." She looked him over some more. "Very charming indeed."

Inspiration struck Katherine. "My friend Lupe assumed Luag was a PenUlt model when she met him."

Kate's eyes didn't depart from Luag. "Did she now?"

Lupe's priest married Katherine and Luag at the end of August. It was a small wedding with just twenty friends and family members, but the scenery made it grand. They had it in the grassy park on the Santa Monica cliffs overlooking the ocean.

"I do," Katherine said, lost in Luag's eyes.

"I do," said he, smiling back at her.

They kissed for five minutes.

Anxious to get started on their honeymoon in the bridal suite at the Miramar, Katherine looked for an escape route, and judging by the way the reserved Luag held onto her, he was looking for one as well.

But they had guests.

Kelsey was there and made a point of shaking Luag's hand, which meant she could bring him into the dream visits. "'Tis verra pleased I am indeed tae meet ye, Luag MacDonald," she said in perfect Gaelic.

"And I ye, Kelsey MacGregor," Luag told her.

Kelsey's phone played a bar of Celtic rock music, making her roll her eyes and sigh. "Sorry, I promised I would take this." Into her phone, she said, "Sarah, I pulled a lot of Celtic University strings to get you that position. You told me you loved it and you wanted to stay, so I pulled even more strings. You don't want to find out what happens if you make me break my promises..."

Katherine turned to Luag, who was also watching Kelsey walk away. "I wonder what that's all about."

He pulled her close to him and kissed her soundly. "I think you have much better things to wonder about, Mrs. MacDonald."

❧

THEY WERE ONLY HOME ON THE WEEKENDS anymore. It was a bit trying, but it would only be for a few years, while Luag was young and in demand as the hot new survival-gear model. Kate had promised him a position at PenUlt after that, along with giving Katherine a few years' leave of absence.

PenUlt's commercials with him had been so popular that Katherine and Luag's phones rang nonstop during business hours with offers to hire him as a model until they broke down and got an answering service.

Katherine was Luag's full-time manager. She

made sure he got the most advantageous deals possible and only modeled for the best companies.

They bought a Scottish-style cottage in Santa Monica. It was so close to PenUlt's headquarters that they could walk, once Luag's modeling career slowed down. But thanks to Luag's earnings, their garage held two new Mercedes convertibles.

The cars stayed in their garage except on the weekends. Every work week, a new limousine took Luag and Katherine to the airport and they flew off to Bali or Peru or some other exotic location for a photo shoot.

They were almost done moving into their cottage. Lupe and Ignacio had helped them find a houseful of handmade furniture, and they brought his kids over every Sunday after church to play in the backyard while Luag barbequed and the cafe was closed. Katherine had taken pleasure in ordering handmade linens and dishes to complete the feel of the place, which Luag assured her felt like home.

The doorbell rang.

Katherine rushed to answer it, eager to meet more of the neighbors, who it turned out they had a lot in common with, all of them being into cottages.

A smiling UPS man greeted her with a huge flat box standing next to him. "Delivery for Luag and Katherine McDonald."

"I'm Katherine MacDonald."

"Will you please sign here? Thanks."

"Can you help me get this inside?"

Luag walked around her and took hold of the large box. "Never ye mind. Thank ye. I've got it from here."

The return address on the box was Kelsey MacGregor at Celtic University, and once it was inside their living room and the door closed, Katherine and Luag eagerly tore it open.

Both of them gasped.

It was a large painting in a beautiful frame suitable for putting over their fireplace. It would fit there exactly, in fact, as if it had been custom-made just for their house.

Which was remarkable.

Because it was a painting of Leif, Jessica, Taran, Lauren, Amena and a man who must be her husband, a dozen people who must be their grown children, and three dozen more who must be their grandchildren.

It had been painted inside Cresh Manor, where Lauren had built several more improvements besides the water closet and the Franklin stove. She had also expanded the place considerably.

Katherine stroked Luag's back. "I'm so glad to see everyone happy and healthy."

He took her into his arms, the two of them still looking at the painting.

"Aye, 'tis good to ken all is well with them."

He kissed her.

"Just as all is well with us."

AFTERWORD

Hi, Jane here.

I hope you enjoyed Luag and Katherine's story. I had fun writing it.

Katherine is modeled after my mom, Junelle, a beautiful, blonde, strong-willed woman who likes the finer things in life. She's part Norwegian, so we come from Viking stock!

The next Dunskey Castle book, Meehall, starts at Celtic University, where Kelsey became a druid and received her dream-walking ability. She's gotten her old faire-friend Sarah a job typing up English translations of Gaelic texts for the university's website.

Sarah's boss at Celtic University plonks an iron bracer on Sarah's desk. It reminds her of one of Kelsey's magic druid dreams. In it, Sarah's ex, Michael (Meehall in Gaelic), used this bracer as a time travel object and was a kilted highlander in 1700s Scotland.

At lunch, Sarah's friends say they're calling in sick tomorrow to attend a local fair. They want her to call in sick too.

Sarah isn't keen on giving the bracer back. She wants revenge on Meehall for breaking up with her and decides to use the bracer to have a bit of fun.

Sarah tells her friends they don't have to call in sick because she's taking them back in time.

"Good one!" they tell her, laughing.

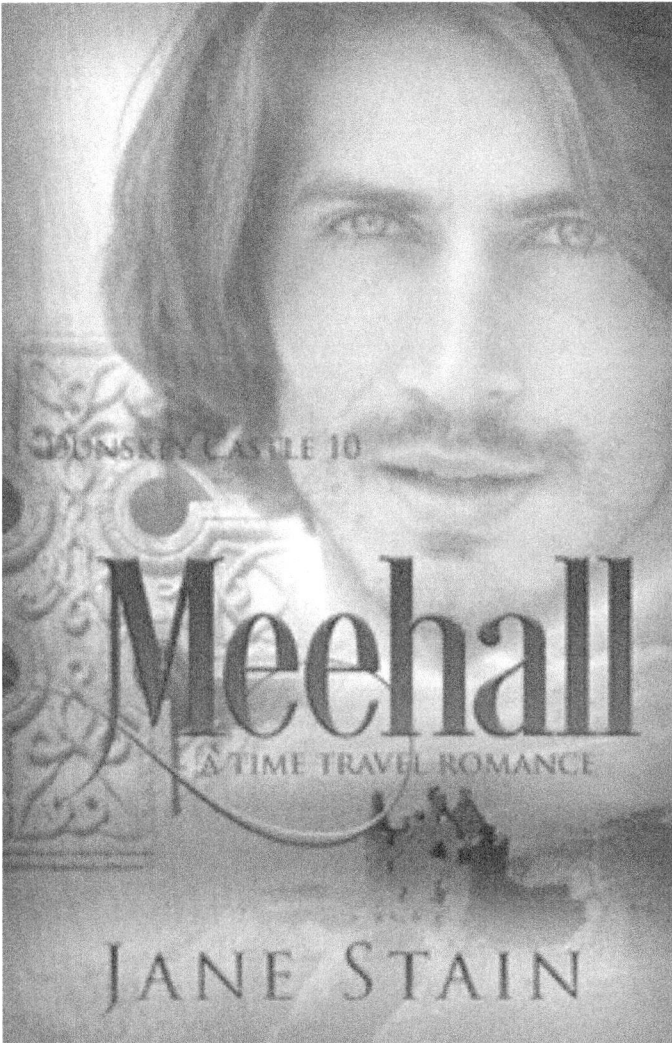

DUNSKEY CASTLE 10

Meehall

A TIME TRAVEL ROMANCE

JANE STAIN

Available only on Amazon.com

Druid Magic - Dunskey Castle 1-3

RenFaire Druids - Dunskey Castle Prequels

Celtic Druids - Dunskey Castle 4-6

Leif - Dunskey Castle 7

Taran - Dunskey Castle 8

Luag - Dunskey Castle 9

Meehall - Dunskey Castle 10

As Cherise Kelley

&

Available everywhere books are sold online

Dog Aliens 1: Raffle

Dog Aliens 2: Oreo

Dog Aliens 3: She Wolf Neya

My Dog Understands English!

High School Substitute Teacher's Guide

Made in the USA
Las Vegas, NV
02 December 2021